THE WILD HUNT

Also By Oskar Jensen

The Stones of Winter

THE WILD HUNT

OSKAR JENSEN

Piccadilly
PRESS

First published in Great Britain in 2016 by
PICCADILLY PRESS
80–81 Wimpole St, London W1G 9RE
piccadillypress.co.uk

A CIP catalogue record for this book is available from the British Library.

ISBN: 978-1-4714-0414-6
also available as an ebook

This book is typeset in 11pt Sabon using Atomik ePublisher

Printed and bound by Clays Ltd, St Ives Plc

Piccadilly Press is an imprint of Bonnier Publishing Fiction,
a Bonnier Publishing company
www.bonnierpublishingfiction.co.uk
www.bonnierpublishing.co.uk

For Charlie Sangster

Say a thing enough times
And have others take heed.
Be it truth or tale,
The thing is done once said.

Leif Ibrahimsson

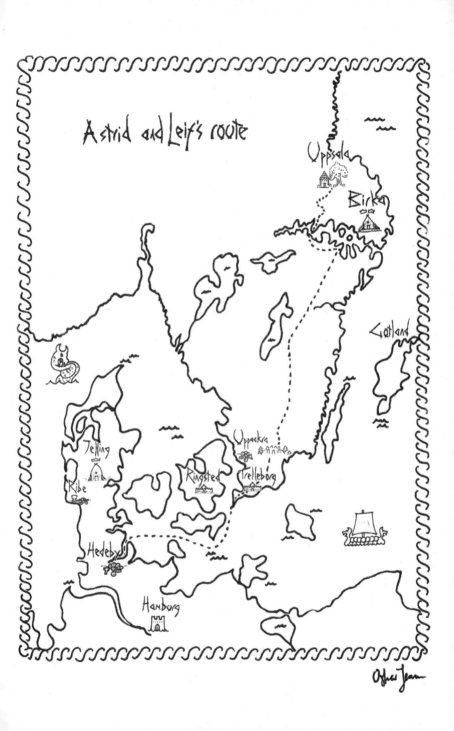

CHAPTER ONE

Denmark, 959 AD

'Go you to the cells and get me Grimnir, the killer, the pagan!' Haralt Bluetooth, new-crowned King of the Danes, fairly snarled out the order. With heavy tread and clink of mail, two huscarls hurried to obey. Shadows were swallowing up the Great Hall at Jelling, and the light of a rust-red sunset arrowing through narrow windows stained the two guards' armour as if with blood as they passed.

The king was left alone with his two councillors: Arinbjorn, a grizzled Norwegian, and Bishop Reginbrand. Tall, fair and wiry, the bishop looked not unlike Haralt himself – though a good deal older than the young king. The advisors exchanged a wary glance.

'Oh, I know what it is you think,' said Haralt. 'Grimnir? What possible use could I have for a man who stands under sentence of death? A priest of Odin, accused of sacrificing human babes? But he is also the best hunter in my kingdom and I hold a noose around his neck; he is mine to command. And there is a service I would have him do me.'

The two men knew better than to protest. Tight-lipped, Arinbjorn strode to a table.

'It grows dark. I'll light some lamps.' With a clack and a fizz, his old hands struck tinder and flint, and soon a yellow pool of oil light spread around the three. Beyond, the hall grew darker. The flickering glow gave their gaunt faces a ghoulish look. And it was in this unearthly light that the two huscarls returned. Marching between them, his wrists bound, was Grimnir.

The group of three halted just below the dais where Haralt stood. Grimnir was so tall that their heads were almost on a level, and the king stared straight into his hard grey eyes. Grimnir stared back, his head unbowed. After a dozen long, measured breaths, Haralt broke the look, frustrated. 'Welcome, Grimnir, the condemned,' he said.

'And greetings to you, Haralt, son of Gorm,' said the prisoner.

Haralt struck him full across the face. 'My name,' he hissed, 'is Haralt Bluetooth, King of the Danes.' He turned half away from the sight of Grimnir's right eye, already beginning to swell from the force of the blow. 'I have a task for you, Grimnir. Do it well and you shall have your freedom.'

'I am listening . . . King Bluetooth.'

'You are the finest tracker and spearman in all my lands, and the least merciful. You have shown yourself willing to kill those younger and weaker than yourself in cold blood.'

2

The bound man's face purpled. 'Lies!' he spat. 'I have never harmed a child, nor killed any that did not come at me sword in hand.'

Haralt waved the protest away. 'Sentence has been passed; your guilt is not in question,' he said. 'It is not to damn you further that I say these things, but to make plain your usefulness. Two outlaws were lately seen trespassing in Jelling. They stole something of great value. Their lives are forfeit. Word has just reached me from Hedeby, down on the coast, where they have been spotted seeking passage to the Swedish court at Birka. I want you to hunt them down: to kill the one, and bring me the other. You shall have men and horses to aid you. Will you do this thing for me, Grimnir?'

They both knew it was not really a question, but a command. For what sort of choice was it, to kill or be killed? Grimnir sighed. 'Their names, lord?'

'One, a boy, is called Leif, known by some as Skald-Leif, for he was my father's poet. The other is a girl. Astrid Gormsdottir.'

ᚠ

'My liege,' said Reginbrand, once Grimnir had been marched away, 'let me go with him, I beg of you. I have always longed to go to Sweden, as the blessed Unni did before me. If I could convert their leading men, even the kings, then he need not have died in vain. Besides, I could keep Grimnir in check, and stop him fleeing into the wilds.'

3

'My good bishop,' smiled Haralt, 'why do you think I am sending armed riders with Grimnir, if not to keep him closely guarded?' He paused, frowning, as if wrestling with a problem. 'But for all that, your zeal does you credit: you shall go with Grimnir. It would suit me well to have fellow Christians in Sweden. Prepare yourself for a hard journey.'

With a low bow of thanks, Reginbrand left the hall.

'So,' said Arinbjorn. 'Astrid and Leif are back. Your headstrong sister and her word-wise little friend. Some nerve, to show themselves here in Jelling so soon after you had them exiled.'

'I should never have been so soft,' said Haralt. 'Who knows what trouble they may make for me in Sweden. She will be plotting with their kings to take my throne, mark my words.'

'You really mean to kill the boy, then?'

'I spoke the truth to Reginbrand,' said the king. 'A Swedish alliance would suit me well. Leif must die. His tongue is too dangerous, and I still suspect it was he, not Astrid, who murdered Bishop Folkmar last winter. But if Astrid wishes to go to their court, then let her!'

'My liege?'

'She shall be seized, her friend will be killed before her eyes, and she will be carried to the Swedes in chains, a gift from one king to another. It will break her will, and put a stopper on any miserable plotting. And I shall have a new friend in the North.'

'If all goes well,' said Arinbjorn. 'To my mind, you risk much by sending Reginbrand. He and Grimnir will be at each other's throats all the way. They'll end up killing each other, like as not, and then where will we be?'

4

Haralt grinned a wide wolf's grin. 'We will be rid of two dangers, that is where. A priest of Odin and a priest of Germany. Reginbrand is a strong ally: perhaps too strong. His loyalty lies more with the Archbishop in Hamburg, and the German king, than with me. If he was to die in Sweden, I'm sure I could find myself another bishop. One of my own.'

Arinbjorn shook his head and whistled. 'You're more cunning than even your father in his prime, sire. You've sent Grimnir on this mission out of wisdom, when I would have sworn, till a moment ago, you were acting out of anger.'

The king gave the old man a long, searching look. At last, he shrugged. 'Goodnight, Arinbjorn.'

'Goodnight, sire.'

Haralt stalked into the royal bedchamber, slamming the oak doors behind him. Alone, he could let out the fury that was churning within him. 'Thieves,' he muttered. 'Murdering little thieves!'

White-knuckled, his trembling hand went to his waist and drew forth a dagger from its jewelled sheath. He stood facing the wall opposite his bed, where two leather straps hung loose from nails. Until recently, they had held the Toledo sword that he had claimed from his father, Gorm the Old. The sword he had used to strike the head from the shoulders of his father's draugur: the undead corpse that had risen from his tomb. But now the sword was stolen. Without noticing what he was doing, Haralt stabbed the dagger into the wooden wall, driving the iron point deep, again and again and again.

CHAPTER TWO

'We never should have taken back the sword,' said Leif. He and Astrid were sitting in a low, dark room, Leif packing a travelling bag, Astrid cutting her own hair.

'We never should have come back at all,' said Astrid. 'We were meant to sail for Iceland, remember? "Iceland or anywhere," that's what we always said. Only *someone* got seasick the first day out of harbour, so now, it's just "anywhere". I'm warning you, you'd better not be sick again when we make the crossing to Sweden.'

'It's just a narrow strait; I'm sure I'll cope,' Leif said, letting her harsh words slide off him. 'It was that great ocean I couldn't stand.' He sighed. 'Now I won't meet Egil Skallagrimsson.'

Last winter, Astrid and Leif had fought against Haralt and his ally Bishop Folkmar. They had fought on behalf of the old ways: for the Yelling Stones, the gods, the trolls and witches and the word-magic that Leif held dear. But they had lost. Leif had shown mercy to Folkmar and in return Folkmar had destroyed the stone circle of Jelling, and then ended up dead of a heart attack. Leif was accused of his murder, and Astrid had sworn she was guilty, to save Leif's life. Banished from the kingdom, they had taken ship to Iceland and now, forced to turn back because of Leif's seasickness, they were fugitives in their own land.

'So it doesn't matter that we took back what was rightfully ours,' Astrid reasoned. 'All right, call it stealing if you like. We're outlaws already, aren't we? And we had to get past Jelling to reach Hedeby . . .'

They had crossed the country mostly by moonlight, two slender figures on a pale horse. At dead of night, they had crept into the hall through a secret entrance to Astrid's old, abandoned room, and Leif charmed open the lock on Haralt's doors. The sword had belonged at one time or another to both their fathers, and neither felt anything but delight at taking it from right under Haralt's snoring nose. 'Besides,' Astrid said, 'I'll need a sword if I'm to be a warrior.'

'You're still bent on trying that disguise then?' said Leif.

'It's *not* a disguise! I really –' Astrid began, but he put a hand to her mouth.

'Hush. I can hear a patrol going past.'

They were keeping their voices low, holed up as they were in a wattle-and-daub shack in the middle of Hedeby, the bustling centre of shipping that Leif had once called home. Now they dropped bag and scissors and flung themselves to the hard earth floor, below the eyeline of the tiny square windows. The tramping of many feet shuddered through their ears. Astrid found some of her own shorn hair tickling her nostrils, and fought back a sneeze. *Silly*, she thought. *It's not a crime to sneeze. We're only in trouble if someone recognises us. No one knows we're here.*

Aloud, she carried on her protest in a whisper. 'I really *do* mean to be a warrior when we get to Birka. If they can make you a skald at the court, they can make me a huscarl.'

The noise of marching died away, and they rose, Astrid still talking. 'There have been shield maidens before. I can fight as well as any boy my age. Better. But since we're outlaws here, we may as well change our appearance.' As she spoke, she worked the scissors, and the last of her long golden tresses fell away, a blonde crop left framing her face. 'How do I look?' she asked.

'Rather like a girl with badly cut hair,' said Leif.

'You're right,' she sighed. 'I suppose I'll have to bind my chest tight to make it flat.'

'Frankly, I'm not sure that's necessary,' he said, eyeing her slim upper body critically.

'A word of advice,' said Astrid, picking up his half-empty bag and ramming it over his head. 'Never be frank.'

And then the door crashed open.

ᛁ

'I've found you a ship!' It was Johanna Svensdottir, the owner of the shack. An old friend of Leif's, she had been the one to turn to when they needed a hideout. Her face glowed with excitement as she carefully closed the door.

8

'Ginnarr the horse-trader has a cargo vessel, the *Klaastad*, bound for Uppaakra on Sweden's west coast. It's a short voyage. He's sailing tonight,' she said.

'Then we can take Hestur?' cried Astrid, clapping her hands. 'I hated the thought of leaving him behind.' Hestur was her stallion. 'And I'm sure he's a far better sailor than Leif.'

'I'll be glad to be rid of him,' said Johanna, 'he's taking up the whole church . . . but be sure to cover him. Haralt's men are on the alert. I'm worried you've been spotted by someone.'

'A good thing we'll be leaving in the dark,' said Leif, who had finally managed to remove the sack from his head.

þ

The streets of Hedeby were empty of all but shadows when Astrid and Leif slipped away. In daylight, the wooden paths echoed to the clamour of a thousand traders, come from the whole world over: fur-swaddled Russians, sweet-scented Arabs, Germans, Englishmen, Finns and Franks. Forges hammered, purses jingled, and the air turned blue with oaths as men and women did business. Hedeby was a town full of money, but with no magic, and Leif, who had spent his whole childhood there, could not love it.

But now, at night, their way lit only by flickering candles glimpsed through polished horn windows, with a growing breeze ghosting through the reeds that grew up from the marsh all around and lone clouds scudding black against the moon – now, for the first time, it was as if something otherworldly *did* stalk these streets. The two friends were wary, on edge. Snatches of song and laughter only just carried to them on bitter-cold air from the taverns up ahead, the merry sounds at odds with their own situation.

'First to the church,' whispered Astrid, as they slipped between shadows. The low wooden building, thatched like the rest, was marked out by a squat bell tower, its summit lost in darkness. A soft whinny greeted them as they unlocked and opened the south-side door. There in the dingy space was Hestur, draped in dirty sackcloth. Astrid ran to him, throwing her arms around the horse's neck whilst Leif stroked his flank and lulled him with calming, secret words. After a moment he turned to Astrid.

'Ready?'

She nodded, guiding Hestur's head round to the door.

And a deep, dry voice spoke out of the night behind them.

'You're sure this is the place they were last seen?' said the voice. It was muffled, and with a swoop of their hearts, the two friends realised it came from *outside* the little church. The speaker must be standing on the other side of the north door.

'Yes, Lord Grimnir,' said another voice, this one cracked and timid.

'Then,' said the first voice, 'this is where the hunt begins.' The door rattled and shook as if under the force of a giant's hand. 'Locked!' the voice said. 'Well, no matter. Do we break it down or burn it?'

Astrid and Leif hardly dared to breathe.

'You forget yourself, Grimnir.' This new speaker's tones were heavily accented, and they both knew he must be a German. 'This is a place of holy worship and you shall not defile it. If it is locked then we must obtain a key.'

'Oh yes, and see our quarry fly,' bit back the one called Grimnir. 'I know you seek an excuse to get across the water, and bring what you call light to those poxed Swedes. But my business, and my burden, is to find . . . and, I suppose, to kill. So, Reginbrand, step away from that door, or must my axe break through both you and it?'

They heard a scuffling of many feet and a rasp of blades, before the timid voice broke in. 'If I might make so bold, masters – there *is* another door. Round the other side . . .'

Astrid seized Leif by the shoulders, her eyes blazing. 'Go!'

Leif hurled himself through the door, rolling to one side. Astrid grabbed Hestur's reins and swung herself half into the saddle, driving a heel into his underbelly, and the stallion bolted, his heavy shoulder knocking splinters from the wood of the door frame. Leif jumped for Astrid's out stretched hand as the great white beast surged past him and they both swarmed up low onto his back, bursting into the air.

'Left!' Leif shouted and Astrid tugged Hestur's head sharply. Behind them rose a clamour of oaths, the bloom of torchlight and 'Stop, in the name of the king!' Craning his neck, Leif could make out a dozen armed and armoured men, most of them milling in confusion, torn between giving chase and turning back to their own mounts. One, a simply enormous man, grey and heavy as an old dog-wolf, came running at them, head down, shoulders all but spanning the narrow alley. As he ran, Leif saw him unsling something long and straight from across his back.

'Down!' Leif screamed, and flattened himself over Astrid's back, forcing her low on Hestur's neck. With a dizzying *whirr*, the man's spear shot past them, thrown with terrifying power. Leif spun, struggling to keep his seat. It was only when he had his balance and could clap a hand to his head that he could understand the sticky hot trickling down his neck: the spear had nicked his ear as it passed. They galloped on, Hestur's hoofs raising a din that rang before them down the wooden streets.

With a bellow of rage, the man wrenched his spear free of the door where it had lodged, still quivering with the impact. 'To horse!' he cried. 'To horse! They will be seeking a ship. Make all speed to the wharf!'

⸙

Ginnarr, captain of the *Klaastad*, turned to his steering-oarsman. 'Cast all loose and set the mainsail. We're leaving.'

The man shot him a puzzled glance. 'But, captain, those two passengers and their horse – they haven't boarded. You'll lose good money on this.'

'Just do it,' Ginnarr said. 'Didn't you hear the shouting? Can't you see the torches? There's trouble in town tonight, and I'll not risk the king's men closing down the harbour. That wind is going to back into the east by morning, mark my words, and we'll never clear the channel.'

That made the man hurry. To be stuck in Hedeby with a full cargo of horseflesh, eating the ship empty and fouling the decks? No fear. He ran forward. 'Make sail,' he shouted. 'You there,' he said, turning to a thrall – a slave – 'haul up the gangplank.'

The thrall, a small girl of the Sami, or Laplanders, grimaced, and bent to the task of lifting in the heavy plank. Muscles straining, she suddenly toppled back as strong hands hauled it in for her. Looking up she saw one of the passengers who *had* made it aboard. He was a thick-bearded Arab, dark-skinned and clad in robes, and now he offered her a large, leathery hand. Smiling, she took it, and rose to her feet. The *Klaastad* was now free, timbers creaking, skittish as a foal on the ebbing tide.

'Thank you, sir,' she said, in a voice as soft as the fall of snow upon pine needles.

'My name is Issar,' he said.

'Mine is Jaska, sir.'

'I mean, you need not call me sir –' He broke off, and wheeled round, as a clatter of hoofs drummed out from the jetty. A massive horse, two riders on its back, was galloping at them, scattering fishing nets and pitching pots into the black water on either side.

'By the Prophet, they mean to jump,' Issar said. The big horse never faltered, launching itself across the gulf between jetty and ship. It made the leap by a whisker, its rear hoofs scrabbling on the ship's strake before hauling itself inboard. The *Klaastad* bucked, dipped, shivered under the impact, and the other horses penned amidships whinnied in alarm.

Ginnarr, his face a storm cloud, staggered across. 'What in Thor's name is going on? Who the Hel are you two?'

Astrid leapt from Hestur's back to the deck. Once again, angry voices were raised behind her. Let them shout: they were on shore, and no ship could be made ready to pursue them until morning. She grinned, and placed a purse of silver in Ginnarr's trembling hand. 'We're your passengers, Captain Ginnarr. Better late than never, eh?'

CHAPTER THREE

Astrid awoke with the change in the wind. All through the night and into the morning she had slept where she fell on deck, moments after handing Ginnarr his money, and Leif had cradled her head and looked, wondering, at a face so peaceful and childlike, that betrayed none of the shock and terror that he knew they had both felt. Were still feeling. Yet Astrid was at peace on the water. The tang of salt on her lips, the whip of spray across her face, the grey depths and the ever-broader sky soothed her like a mother's touch. More, in fact, than she could ever have said for her mother . . .

'The wind's changed,' she said, rising to her feet. Even Leif, no sailor, had noticed: the brisk, regular motion of the ship had given way to sluggish bucks and wallows. They no longer seemed to be moving past the low-lying land that stretched, distant, to either side. The creaking of the timbers and the *flap-crack* of the sail were growing, and it irritated him.

'Yes,' said Ginnarr, from where he stood next to the steering-oar. 'And we've no rowers to drag us against it.

The *Klaastad*'s a good little craft, but she can't point up far into a headwind, and even with the prevailing current pulling us along the Belt, we'll be hard-pressed, tacking in so little sea room, to hold station, never mind making any headway . . .'

'I have *no* idea what he just said,' Leif muttered to Astrid.

She ignored him. 'Captain,' she said. 'If, say, another ship was following us, and it *did* have rowers . . . How long would it take them to catch us – I mean, to catch us up?'

Ginnarr raised his shaggy eyebrows so high they nearly disappeared beneath his woollen hat. 'I'm no fool, boy. With us stuck with the wind in our teeth, your pursuers, whoever they are – which is none of *my* business, see – they could overhaul us by nightfall. If they're in a well-manned longship, as I've a hunch they might be. And that'd be bad for me too, what with more time wasted. I'll see if anyone aboard can pray us up a wind.' And he stumped off forward.

Leif's face, already green, went greener.

Astrid was beaming. 'Hear that?' she said. 'He called me boy. I *am* a master of disguise!'

That gave Leif the strength to muster his own smile, before tottering after Ginnarr. A small circle of crew and passengers was clustered at the foot of the mast, just aft of the horse pen.

'Which way is east?' asked Issar, the traveller. Ginnarr pointed wearily ahead, and Issar knelt, hands clasped, intoning words in a language Leif found both strange and beautiful.

Astrid laid a hand on his shoulder. 'What is it?' she asked.

'That must be Arabic. My father's tongue,' said Leif. 'I've never heard it spoken before now.'

'If he's praying for a change in the wind, it's not working,' said Astrid. The easterly breeze was if anything growing stronger. Others clearly felt the same: one crewmember was scratching at the mast with a knife, another whispering under his breath in what sounded like Latin. Ginnarr aimed a kick at the little Lapland thrall. 'You, Jaska, your people are good with magic. Can't you whistle us a wind?'

The girl clutched her arms about her chest and shook her head swiftly. 'I know only forests. The sea scares me.'

'Useless little thing,' said Ginnarr. 'Or maybe not quite useless. If nothing else works, I could throw you overboard as an offering to Njord the sea god . . .'

Astrid dug Leif in the ribs. 'Do something,' she whispered.

'I don't feel so well,' he said.

'You'll feel worse in a minute.'

He knew when to heed a threat. Turning his face to the now biting wind, he gathered his thoughts.

'Dancer on the sea's roof,
Shaper of the sand dunes.
Moaner, light-tipped scudder;
Mover of the mountains.
Constant friend of seabirds,
Foe of fir on hillside,
Hurrier of tempests,
Temperer to cliff face . . .'

Astrid hung back. He was singing the wind, calling to its heart, and she knew better than to interrupt. Casting about for distraction, she glanced aft.

Far in their wake, low against the landscape, she saw a dark speck upon the water. From it rose what had to be a mast, bearing no sail. A longship, then, rowed by many oarsmen. Of course, it was a busy sea lane; why should there not be a ship? But then again, why would any merchantman put to sea in the face of such a headwind? Astrid bit her lip. For the first time in months, perhaps since her father's corpse had risen, red-eyed, in the stifling burial chamber, a knot of fear tightened in her stomach.

Leif was still speaking, back straight, arms spread and raised, face jutting up into the wind. It seemed to be circling around him. The *Klaastad* slewed and groaned uncertainly, and the man at the steering-oar swore in dismay as he tried to hold some kind of course. Ginnarr hollered back at him. 'Keep her head up, curse you, or we're done for! Better ships than ours have been wrecked between these islands.'

Each word Leif spoke was at once whipped away, the wind greedy for his voice. Astrid could catch only snatches.

'. . . *you and I have shared, and*
How we both know hunger . . .
. . . honour patience, yes, but
Lulls and palls are past now . . .
. . . Gird yourself for blowing.
See friend: the sky screams, "East!"'

And she could have sworn she saw that wind become a living thing: a silvered, shuddering animal, long-limbed and graceful, and she saw Leif gather it up in his arms as you might a bundle of washing, but as tenderly as you might a baby, or a lamb. And he seemed to clutch that living wind a moment, two, to his beating chest, and lay his cheek upon it, before hurling it out into the fresh grey sky.

On the instant, the sail filled and billowed, all ropes going rigid, and the clamour of flaps and creaking turned to the eager hum of a well-tuned instrument. A shout rose from the sailors. The bickering horses went quiet. And Leif slumped, spent and slack. Astrid barely caught his shoulders before he hit the deck.

Leif's eyes were closed in sleep. The crew were trimming the sail. The other passengers exchanged glances of wonder. Astrid kept glancing behind her, where the black ship had slipped back out of sight. And Ginnarr's keen, weathered eyes were narrowed in thought, as he stared at the boy who had sung them a wind.

ᚱ

Dawn, and the world was drained of colour, the sun's white-gold fingers hesitant and bashful as they started to trace the eastern edges of the sky's rim. Grey sea, grey sky, grey land away to larboard, as grey as the knife that Leif found at his throat. Slowly, he struggled up from the depths of sleep, bleary, groggy.

Ginnarr's craggy features lowered over him.

'Up, boy,' he said. 'We need the wind to veer. We've gone south about Ringsted in record time; but if this gale of yours doesn't shift we'll be blown all the way to Bornholm – her timbers won't take a broad reach up the Oresund in this, with all those waves slamming her amidships.'

'Oh, why can't you just talk normal Danish?' Leif said, coming fully awake. If he kept Ginnarr calm, this might not be too serious. Where was Astrid? 'Besides, a thing like that takes all my strength. I'd need maybe a day before I could . . .'

'Not good enough,' said Ginnarr. Behind him stood three burly sailors, arms folded. 'You're my magic charm, you are, see, and you're going to harness us a wind if it kills you.' He paused. 'Which will be a better fate than what I've got in store if you fail.'

Leif's eyes were flickering about, searching for Astrid, but he couldn't see past the crewmen who were closing in on him.

ᚱ

Astrid was right forward, expertly balanced in the very prow of the ship. They had crept north-east during the night, and their destination, the trading port of Uppaakra, lay just hidden over the horizon. Before them, some way off, a low spit of sand and reefs jutted out into the channel. She felt her face washed with the first rays of pale gold, felt the play of her new-cropped hair as it whipped about her face, felt the shift of wood and water beneath her lightly placed feet. The *Klaastad's* prow cut a clear deep channel through the grey sea, washes of white water rinsing away her recent cares. She stretched her arms out sideways, hopped over the hit of the largest waves, dancing with the ship and the sea. In her ears were the whistle of wind, thump of sail, call of seabirds. The earthy, healthy smell of horses from behind her was familiar, comforting. Maybe they could just sail on, forever? But no, there was Leif, he was no sailor . . . She turned to see if he was awake, and saw Leif being hauled to his feet, a knife at his neck. The sudden jolt of a heavy wave sent her reeling against the prow, and she fell into the sacks of luggage bundled beneath.

'Ow!' she said, her voice low. Her hip had caught on something sharp, stuck in the corner of their knapsack. Her harp, the one that Leif had made her. And now he was in danger. *Think, Astrid, think*, she told herself. He was at the mercy of a tough gang of sailors. She was lying fallen on her bum, hidden from the action by a small herd of tethered horses, with nothing but a harp . . . A harp . . .

Ginnarr was bellowing at Leif now, the words carrying to where she lay. 'I'm making you my thrall. You and that pretty girl – don't think you fooled me with that disguise – you're going to sing me up whatever wind I want. I'm sure we can think of a use for her too, right, lads? But it'll go much easier for both of you if you talk this wind into the south, *right now*.'

Astrid had stopped listening, bending her fingers to the unpicking of the sack. She drew forth the harp, checking it anxiously for any signs of damage. None, only that the horsehair strings, woven from strands of Hestur's tail, were slack. Swiftly, she wound the amber tuning pegs, thrusting aside the memories that rose in her mind as she did so. If she was to work her own weather-magic, she couldn't afford a single stray thought.

Ginnarr's shouts had stirred the other passengers. Issar, the tall Arab, tried to lever his way between two beefy Danes. 'Captain Ginnarr, what is all this uproar? What are you doing to that boy?'

'Whatever I like,' shot back Ginnarr, red-faced. 'He's my property now.'

Astrid fit the curve of her back to the curve of the prow, settling against the wood, eyes on the sky and fingers on her harp strings. Almost idly she began to pick the second, third and fifth of its five strings, just those three notes again and again, falling into the rhythm of wave and wind. The sound shimmered, bright, hesitant, hopeful: morning music. Her fingers, stiff and clammy from breeze and spray, began to warm and loosen.

'Really,' Issar said, his own voice rising, 'I must protest. That boy has paid his way, just as we have. Can we all expect the same treatment – to wake with the bonds of slavery about our wrists?'

'You don't have to expect anything, outlander,' said Ginnarr. 'The sooner this boy gets us blown to Uppaakra, the sooner you can drag your stinking hide off my ship!'

Without changing the beat, Astrid shifted her fingers down, now striking the first, third and fourth strings, over and over. The sound was still beautiful, but it had deepened, strengthened. She felt the wind upon her upturned cheeks. Was it just her, or was that growing too?

'But he stays, I suppose?' Issar brought his face close to Ginnarr's. 'And I took you for an honest trader! You're a common Viking, Ginnarr.'

'Viking?! How dare you? I'm no pirate,' said Ginnarr, stung by the insult. 'But my word is law on board my own vessel.'

'And the law's purpose is to provide justice! I've seen the way you treat your thralls,' Issar said. 'A pirate *and* a tyrant!' One or two crewmen shifted, laying hands on hilts or the handles of axes.

Astrid doubled the speed of her picking, working the three middle strings roughly. In the west behind them, dark clouds were massing, low to the skyline. The wind had risen to a gale now, unheeded by the *Klaastad*'s crew. Astrid rose from where she sat, harp braced on her left hip, and slashed her fingers three times across all five strings. Thunder roiled and rumbled in the ship's wake, and the horses whickered in fear, stamping their hoofs. It was working. But was it enough? Astrid tossed her head. Leant back. And opened her mouth.

Ginnarr spat at Issar's feet and the Arab trader went for him, swinging with both fists. The old sailor jerked Leif up as a shield and all three went reeling. There was a dull gleam of wicked metal: Ginnarr's knife. And then the lightning cracked behind them and they all turned and saw.

There was a figure standing in the bows, straddling the prow itself, raised high above the stirring horses and the clashing waves. It was lithe and beautiful, haloed with the gold of a rising sun, swaying as one with the gathering tempest. With one hand it struck at a shining harp, and its head was thrown back in a wild, wild song. Some saw an angel, some a jinn, some a Valkyrie. And Leif, head still spinning from Issar's blow, saw that it was Astrid and he smiled.

Astrid felt her chest and throat swelling with the song of the storm, and her voice rose to a shriek higher than the gale in the rigging. Every bit of her was thrilling to that song, and she felt what she knew Leif must sometimes feel: connected. She was the wind, and she was the rain. Then for an instant she glanced over her shoulder, away from the goggling crowd. With both hands she brandished her harp aloft, a trophy against the sky. Then she jumped high, aiming her fall onto the soft sacks beneath, so that she was in the air at the exact moment that the world shuddered and cracked, as the *Klaastad* ran full upon the Trelleborg reefs.

CHAPTER FOUR

Leif swayed up to his knees, ice grey Baltic sea already streaming in around them. The world was askew, a rocking blur of thundering surf and slantwise deck. A foaming white roller crashed over him, tumbling him back and filling his mouth with salt water. All about was the din of scrabbling feet, scrabbling hoofs, big men seeking holds, seeking escape.

Through the spray, a small female hand. He grasped at it and was hauled up.

'Astrid,' he said, and blinked: not her, but a tiny slip of a girl, dark hair, pale eyes, small smile. A sailor blundered by, swearing, and the *Klaastad* heaved over a little further. Leif wiped the heavy water from his eyes with his free hand, whilst the girl tugged at the other. 'This way,' she said.

Astrid had landed a moment after impact, missing the shock. Snatching their packs, she stuffed in the harp and drew the blue-steeled sword. At a stroke, she cut the rope mesh holding back the horses. Uncertain, they milled about, fighting to keep their footing.

'Leif!' she called, and then she saw him, running towards her, hand in hand with that little thrall. A bolt of pain ran through her at the sight, so fleeting that she missed it. But now she was boosting him onto the back of a dappled grey mare. 'Come on – we're off!' she bawled at him, swinging herself onto Hestur's back, cursing the lack of a saddle.

Leif, half mounted on the strange horse, looked in confusion, first at Astrid, then at the other girl, now battling against the mounting froth of sea. Astrid breathed, once, then shrugged herself off Hestur's back and heaved the girl onto a bay colt close by.

'Anyone else?' she said – and sighed, as the long-robed Arab hauled himself onto a horse, landing a hefty kick in the chest of a Danish sailor as he did so. Astrid climbed back up, stroked Hestur's quivering neck, urged him round to face the gap in the ship's broken side. 'Fly, Hestur!' she cried, digging her heels into his belly.

Ginnarr was braced against the mast, letting wave upon wave pummel his broad back, staring at the gutted hull that had been his pride. With an awful groan, his ship yawed over again, on the point of slipping beneath the tide. A clatter from behind made him turn, to see four horses rising from the surf. 'Oh *skita*!' he yelled, flinging himself to one side, ducking just under the hoofs of the nearest, a big white stallion. Sprawling, drenched, on the deck, he saw the four horses leaping, a cresting wave of animal greater and more graceful than any wave yet. They surged free of the drowning ship, clear of the rolling sea, landing in the breakers of the shallow sand beyond. For a moment, as they filled his sight, the horses – *his* horses – had blotted out the sun.

✝

Grimnir narrowed his iron-grey eyes, the right still inflamed from Haralt's blow.

'Christ-man,' he called, 'come look at this.'

Reginbrand lurched across the deck from the starboard bulwark, where he had been retching into the heaving sea, to where Grimnir stood in the bows. He wiped his mouth with a soaked-through sleeve. 'What, outlaw?'

Grimnir ignored the insult. 'Over there, away to larboard – no, to the *left*, bishop – in the distance. See that dark lump against the headland? It looks like a wreck.'

Reginbrand glanced in the direction Grimnir was pointing. 'Rocks,' he said.

'There are no rocks on the Trelleborg sand spit. That's what takes careless sailors unawares,' said Grimnir.

The German priest struggled to raise his voice above the gale. 'All the more reason to steer well out to sea. If it is a wreck, we hardly wish to risk the same fate ourselves.'

'But it could be *them*!'

'It's out of the way for Uppaakra,' said Reginbrand. 'They'll be there by now. No: we use this wind to keep on for Birka. That's where they're headed, after all – the dockhands we questioned told us as much.'

Grimnir's face tightened at the memory. 'Only after I'd introduced them to my knife . . . I still think you should have let me try the Svensdottir woman. She might have known more.'

'What, let you torture an honest Christian?' Reginbrand's sickly face flushed with colour. 'You would do well, prisoner, to think less on sins you could not commit, and more on those you did. Those murdered children, for example . . .'

'I swear I *never* –'

Reginbrand held up one hand, the other gripping fast to a stay. 'No need to swear, Grimnir, let us not add profanity to your list of crimes. We both know the truth of your bloody past.' He lowered his voice. 'Can you remember their faces? Do those poor souls cry out for your repentance?'

Grimnir twitched, one hand hovering over his sword-hilt. Then he mastered himself, and turned from Reginbrand, his eyes back on the possible wreck, now fading fast astern. Reginbrand's mouth curled up at the corner in a secret smile. Above them, a grey sail billowed. The hunters sailed on.

†

Four sets of hoofs slapped into wet sand as the horses tore across the dunes. Leif urged his mount closer to Hestur, out in front, and called to Astrid. 'Where now? Should we bear north for Uppaakra?'

She shook her head. 'No need – it's not on the way any more. Besides, I've been there before; they've got this great big temple to Odin. And you're not exactly on the best of terms with the one-eyed god.'

Leif thought back to his confrontation with Odin's raven, and the threats he had made. 'You're right,' he said. 'But if not there, then where? Along the coast? But that could take us weeks.' He winced, as an especially heavy jolt from his horse shot through his thighs and backside. 'And any shortcut would be most welcome!'

Astrid, practically at one with Hestur, couldn't help a tiny smirk at his predicament. 'That would mean going through the great forest,' she said. 'We're strangers here; we'd never find the way.'

'I could!' It was the dark-haired girl. Surprised, Astrid and Leif slowed their horses, and she drew up alongside them. 'I can find a way through any wood. I can follow paths in the stars and the sun, and I know the great game-trails north like I know the veins on my arm! The elk-roads are mostly better than those of men if you're looking to get somewhere quickly. And I owe you that much, since it's thanks to you I'm free. If you're headed north, I'd like to come. That way lies my home.' She broke off, blushing, surprised at her own daring at making such a speech.

Astrid beamed. 'I'm Astrid. What's your name?'

'Jaska.'

'You owe us nothing, Jaska. But we'd be glad of the company. And of the help. If you can guide us swiftly through this forest, then you may just have saved Leif's bottom from an untimely end.'

'As for that,' said Issar, coming up on the other side, 'we can purchase saddles and harness in Trelleborg – as well as provisions.' He patted a large purse that swung from his belt. 'I've plenty of silver dinars to go around.'

'You too?' said Astrid.

'Why not?' he replied. 'Birka is as good a place as anywhere in Sweden for a trader. And a wealthy merchant always needs companions, if only for protection.' He gave Leif a hard, searching look as he said all this, and the boy lowered his eyes, though he didn't know why.

'It looks as if we have a company,' Leif said, for want of anything better.

'And a common purpose,' said Astrid, 'which for now mostly involves getting as far away from Ginnarr and his men as possible. Which way, Jaska? North already?'

The little girl shook her head. 'Still east for now,' she said. 'At least as far as Trelleborg itself. The wet sand makes for easy riding, after all.'

'East it is,' said Astrid. 'And I don't know about your bones and bums, but it'll be safest for our heads if we go at a gallop.' And she spurred Hestur forward.

The others exchanged a glance. Groaned, muttered, sighed. Then kicked their heels into their mounts, and sped after the galloping girl. The four horses coursed across the sands. Behind them was the thunder; ahead, the swallowing sun.

CHAPTER FIVE

'Is she all right?' whispered Jaska.

Leif nodded. 'Sometimes she gets a bit carried away. A good night's sleep will set us all to rights.'

Jaska looked less than convinced. But she could take a hint, and moved off, bedding down next to her sleeping horse, resting her back against it. The large beast gave warmth, and shelter. But it also snored.

Leif turned his attention back to Astrid, pale and shivering in two layers of blankets. The pair of them were camped in the sand dunes outside Trelleborg, lying low, whilst Issar bought supplies and riding gear for the journey. 'Best to keep a low profile,' Astrid had said, and she had been right. She'd done so well, but now she was quivering, hot brow and clammy palms, somewhere on the edge of sleep and fever. Leif looked at her. He ached in every limb; there were red marks on his neck where Ginnarr had grasped him; he was tired as any dog could be. But she had led them all that day, poured her will into their escape, and played herself half to death summoning the storm. No wonder that now, she trembled.

He retrieved their knapsack, shook out the harder items upon a tussock, packed it full with clumps of grass and reeds. It wasn't much of a pillow, but it would have to do.

Astrid saw Leif, dim against the moon, standing over her with something heavy in his hands. Everything was dark, and blurred, and wrong. 'Don't hit me,' she screamed.

And she flinched away from him, thrashing about uselessly in the hollow of sand where she lay.

'Shh,' said Leif, trying to soothe her. She was so weak that it was easy to raise her head, and support it with the bolster. The fight went out of Astrid in one ragged breath and she lay quiet and still. He stroked her cheek, her hair. But there were tears in his eyes. He had struck her once before, and Astrid had forgiven him that betrayal. But not, it seemed, forgotten.

He bent close to her ear.

'Sleep, sweet shield maiden.
Softly night unknits you;
Let these cares and cankers
Creep off to the gloaming.'

He sat there by her head for he knew not how long, spinning out his poem, verse after verse, and slowly, slowly, the tension seeped from her limbs and she relaxed into a deep, true sleep.

'Leif,' someone was whispering. 'Leif!'

He looked up. Issar was back, his horse heavy-laden; Leif had not noticed. He blinked, smiled. 'Success?' he said.

'Success,' said Issar. 'And I met a man called Ormulf. Massive. Hairy. And the smell! I don't think much of these

Swedes. But he told me of a shortcut through the forest – gave me a landmark. All because I bought some dried meats from him. Not the sort you'd let your daughter marry, but very friendly.'

'Ormulf,' muttered Leif. 'Strange name.' But he was asleep before he had finished the thought.

|

In the morning they turned inland, buoyant on new-saddled horses. As dune turned to scrub around them, the mewl of seabirds fell away, and their noses were full of fresh scents. Heather, pine, moss, no longer kelp and salt. And then, before them, was the forest.

A stretch of green meadow, strewn with yellow flowers, ran away from them up a gentle hill. Then came the treeline, a dark green blur of spruce and fir. A narrow opening where a dirt track split the trunks. Further back, oaks and forest pines overtopped the lower trees, a spreading canopy of noble branches. Beyond that – who knew? – but it might as well go on forever.

Astrid glanced round at the others. As she expected, Issar's face was clouded: doubt, wonder, the fear of the unknown. Jaska's little eyes were bright and eager. But it was Leif who surprised her. As he gazed at the forest, a look of total longing stole across his features. What was this? The city boy, the mead-hall poet, a secret lover of the woods? She wondered if even he had known this, till now. For her own part, Astrid was uncertain. Her adventures had taught her that danger hid among these wonderful trees. And a Danish forest was one thing. Her land was small; the trees had an end. This was Sweden. The forest was darker. Wilder. And much, much bigger.

Still, Birka lay on the other side, and with it, her chance for fame and fortune: a fresh start. And who knew whether Haralt's men were still on their tail? They might have found Ginnarr by now; they could be riding to Trelleborg. She took a deep breath of fresh, meadow air – perhaps the last for many days. 'Come on,' she said, and spurred Hestur towards the trees.

Leif was the first to follow, eyes fixed on the gap ahead where the path entered the woods. Jaska fell in behind, Issar bringing up the rear. He cast a rueful glance over his shoulder, at the bright, clean space they were leaving. Out of the corner of one eye, he thought he saw a low, dark shape, streaking past them away to their left. A man? A dog? Or probably, he told himself, just their own shadow on the hillside, flickering in the morning sun. They were headed into a land of shadows. It would never do to get jumpy about a single one. He chuckled. This northern land was odd enough already – no need to make it stranger.

†

Noon, and the high sun splintering through the canopy, shafts of light cross-hatching the woody dark. The forest thrummed with insects' wings; the high hall of branches above rang with birdsong. Ferns edged the narrow path, brushing their horses' flanks, hoof beats dampened to a gentle thud by last autumn's carpeting of pine needles, soft from winter and shot through by stray grasses. Jaska leapt from her mount and, barefoot, ran alongside, moss springing and squadging damp between her toes, beneath her heels. This was too far south for her to feel she was home. But it was a start. No one talked much. They were too happy.

ᚼ

A rest by a babbling spring, coursing down a cleft between tussocks of peat, tangled with tree roots. Gratefully, the horses lowered their heads to the trickling water, long noses bumping the year's first forget-me-nots, bright blue bursts of scent and colour. Crumbs of oatcakes and a hard, nutty cheese left for birds and voles to tussle over later. Astrid let Jaska thread some of the flowers through her hair, though it was still too short and most fell out. Issar's deep voice carried well beneath the trees, as he said, 'Ormulf told me we'd be at the place by nightfall. We can make camp there.' Their pace was easy. No one thought much of pursuers any more.

ᛁ

Night fell faster among the trees, and soon their steady trot was reduced to a walk, a single file of four with Jaska, in front, bearing one torch, and Issar, at the rear, another. With the dark, the mesh of birdsong that had engulfed them all day disappeared, but no night noises took their place. Not a scratch, not a snuffle, not a hoot or a howl. The stillness was eerie. Issar raised his voice, calling to Leif in front of him. 'I say, skald, what about a few words to lift the mood? I'm near spooked here, never knowing what might be at my back.'

Leif swivelled in his saddle, dropping his pace still further to bunch his horse alongside Issar's. 'I'm sorry, friend, my mind was on our rest, and not the picking out of stirring lines.'

'Oh, I wasn't asking for a poem, lad, just some conversation!' said Issar.

'That, at least, I think I can give you,' said Leif, darting a glance at the trader, his face half hidden beneath the hood of his robes. There was something almost familiar about that face.

'For one thing,' said Issar, 'it strikes me as odd that here we are, four riders in the wilderness, and all we know of each other are our first names. Not so much as a sire's name between us.' He paused, as if waiting for Leif to speak, but the boy stayed silent. Issar went on. 'Maybe it's for the best – we all seem to be outlaws of one kind or another. An escaped thrall, a foreigner . . . maybe first names are more fitting after all. What do you think?' And he eyed Leif from under the heavy cloth.

Leif flushed. He felt a swoop within him as his stomach dropped away. Was there a hidden meaning in the Arab's words? 'Issar' could easily be an assumed name, after all. It even sounded a bit like Ibrahim. Travellers *did* change their names, when they had a past to conceal. Heart pounding, he said at last, 'As for me, I've kept my sire's name secret. A year ago, I gained the name Skald-Leif, hiding my father's name to make my own. But –'

'Perhaps,' said Issar, his words heavy, 'your father did something to shame his name? It is rare indeed for a son not to bear the name of their sire, among my people as among yours. Though . . . though it may be that our peoples are not so different? Your face, your skin, are not as these lily-white northerners.'

Leif's head was growing dizzy. Why was it suddenly so hard to keep his seat? 'In truth, there are those who would call it shame,' he said, very quietly. 'For you see, I never knew my father. He left my mother before I was born.'

'I understand,' said Issar, very grave. 'That sounds a most dishonourable thing to do. And if there's one thing I've learnt on my travels, it's that honour counts for much among the Norsemen. Who would want a father like that?'

Leif frowned. That wasn't what he had meant at all. He wetted his lips, trying to choose his words more carefully. He said –

'We're here!' came a shout from ahead – it was Jaska – and then Astrid's voice.

'Oh *Hel*,' she said.

'What is it?' said Leif quickly, prompting his horse forward, away from Issar.

'This "landmark" that Ormulf said we'd find,' said Astrid. 'Well – see for yourself.' Then Leif was alongside her, and did see.

The path broadened out into a wide clearing, trees hacked back to make space, in the centre of which rose a low hill, open to the sky. A full moon had risen, unseen till now, and its pale, ghostly light fell full upon that hill. At its crest was a group of what Leif at first took for figures – massive, squat figures, lumpen and still. Then he realised. It was a stone circle.

CHAPTER SIX

Nine stones, jagged and broad, hunched their shoulders on the hilltop. Leif gasped.

'Not again,' he said.

'Not again what?' said Jaska.

Astrid and Leif exchanged a wary glance. Astrid spoke. 'This isn't our first run-in with standing stones. Last time . . . let's just say it didn't end well.'

'But what do they mean?' said Issar. 'They're just stones – aren't they? A landmark. Though why they're out here, in the forest . . .'

'Stones are raised at sites of ancient worship,' said Leif. 'People have been praying here for years – hundreds, perhaps – and that gives them power. They're potent places. *Dangerous* places.' He was frowning, trying to concentrate. His head was filled with a memory from Jelling: the sound of the three stones there, screaming. 'Wait here,' he said. 'I'll see if it is safe.' And he swung himself out of his saddle, in something like a single movement, and handed the reins to Jaska.

Astrid's mouth was a hard line, but she didn't move to stop him. This was his world, not hers. All the same, she nudged Hestur in front of the other horses, and felt for the hilt of the Toledo sword. She would be ready. Behind her, Issar and Jaska held their torches high, glancing around. The blitheness of the day's riding was forgotten.

'If it *is* safe,' Astrid said, 'then this hilltop will make an excellent camp. That's probably why Ormulf suggested it.' But even she could hear the words ring hollow.

Leif crept slowly up the grassy slope. His palms were twitching, and there was a needling at the top of his nose, between his eyes, as if he were about to get a bad cold. There was magic about this place, it hung heavy, and something else – a smell, he thought, a sharpness, a rankness. He couldn't place it, but it wasn't anything good. His feet dragged. The last thing he wanted was to reach that grim circle.

As he crested the mound, a broad bank of cloud slid across the moon. Now the only light came from the amber flicker of two torches, behind him. Dark on darker, their outlines lost, the stones became monstrous to his mind. Then the first was looming up before him, horribly close.

Just a stone. He eyed it up and down, searched its dull, bare face for signs of magic, found none. He hesitated.

Astrid, watching, gripped the sword-hilt tight, her knuckles whitening. The last time she had watched Leif step inside just such a circle, he had vanished, only to emerge in flames, unconscious. She had thought him dead. Now, peering into the black, she could just see his slender form on the edge of the ring. He moved, and she tensed, a shout ready on her lips.

Leif took a slow pace. Another. He was inside the stone circle. And nothing had changed. His flesh was crawling, but that was fear and cold, nothing more. He risked a glance over his shoulder: the others were still there, waiting. Emboldened, he began to move around the circle. But it was now too dark to make out the next stone clearly.

He unpinned a clasp of his tunic, bringing the small metal disc close to his lips.

'Mirror-shard of sun flash, silver midday winker,' he whispered. 'Try hard to remember; taste that light in darkness.' The little brooch flashed bright, not quite as if catching the noon sun, but giving enough of a glow for Leif to see the stone plainly.

Before him was a wolf. A cruel, low-bellied, boar-toothed wolf with skeletal, three-clawed feet and twisting snakes uncoiling from its ears. He almost dropped the clasp, reeling back from the sight. *A picture*, he told himself, *it's just a picture, carved into the rock, its outlines picked out in deep red paint. Although* . . . Screwing up his courage, he leant in close to the stone, sniffing. Was that . . . ? With a trembling finger, Leif touched the image – then leapt away, shocked by a jolt of power that had run right through him. His fingertip burned, and instinctively he put it in his mouth. It tasted as he'd feared it would – the familiar metallic tang of blood.

High up above, something stirred, a ruffling and beating a long way off.

Holding the glowing brooch out in front of him, Leif wheeled around. Other stones, other pictures, sprang up out of the darkness. A man, glassy-eyed, bearing a wicked axe. Another wolf, ears pricked, snakes spewing from its open maw. And a third wolf, bony as the first, a snake in its jaws and a witch on its back. The blood had run on this last stone, and it glistened in the glimmering light. Still wet – it was fresh!

Leif lurched about the circle, the blood throbbing in his temples, heart hammering. What was this place? As he turned, half tripping, towards the ninth stone, the light strengthened, the full moon sloughing off the clouds. In the strange, unearthly brightness, he saw that this one was different. Lower, weirder, all knobbles and rounds. And then it rose and turned towards him, and it was a man.

A scream withered within Leif's throat as he stood, rooted to the spot. The man rose up and up, towering over the boy, shaggy, grey. His eyes were yellow slits, his mouth a red slash filled with fangs. Incredibly, snakes were slithering from beneath the ragged openings of clothing at his neck, at his shoulders. And as the moonlight seared into him, Leif could see his ears begin to sharpen, his nose to lengthen. And his hands – but they weren't hands any longer.

The werewolf threw back its head in a savage howl, a howl that echoed, ragged and raw, from each of the eight stones. That howl brought Leif halfway to his senses, and he turned, ready to throw himself aside as the werewolf gathered itself to spring. But there was a thundering din in his ears and a brutal, more than human force drove into his shoulder from behind and sent him spinning to the ground.

He tried to rise, to turn, but the pain shot through his back and pinned him. Struggling against it, he hauled himself round the other way. He heard a snarl, a snort, and a rushing, singing sound that he'd known once before. Then he was up, at last, and saw, and it was Astrid, wheeling Hestur round towards him. The big white horse picked up its hoofs, stepping high over something that lay writhing on the ground. It was a body. And there, rolling away down the slope into darkness, was its head.

His eyes caught Astrid's as they flashed above him. She had never looked more beautiful, or more terrible. One hand held the sword that had belonged to both their fathers, now dripping gore. The other was reaching for him, and he seized it, hauling himself through gritted teeth up onto Hestur's back. He clutched his arms about her as he had before – it seemed so long ago, another awful night in the fenlands. 'Astrid,' he began.

'No.' She shook her head. 'It's not over.'

And he tore his eyes from her, to look about the circle. From behind each and every stone, a wolf was rising.

ß

With a clatter and stomp, Issar and Jaska were with them, the horses surging up to mill around the hilltop, an urgent knot of hoof and muscle. Issar leant over to Leif. 'Can you ride?' he asked. Leif managed a nod, and the older man reached out with brawny, capable arms, lifting him bodily from Hestur and into Leif's own saddle. Now four horses pointed outward, flanks bunching together. The fear was streaming off them, the scent and the sweat of it, eyes and nostrils wide. Astrid wished, over and over, that her brother Knut were here. He would have swatted a wolf aside with each swipe of his fists. But he had left her, left her and died, as her father had done, and her mother had left as well, and there was only her, and if she did not concentrate, then she too would be dead. She tightened her grip on her blade, glinting silver and slick red in the moonlight. Issar was brandishing a curved sword of his own, with a wicked edge. But the others were unarmed save for the two unwieldy torches. They would have to trust to their horses' hoo—

And the wolves were on them. To Leif, still dazed and struggling for breath, it was as if the night itself had been smashed apart, sending great black shards hurtling towards him. One snarling beast leapt for him, but his horse, rearing of its own accord, dealt it a glancing blow on one massive shoulder with a kicking foreleg and the brute fell back, ragged and panting. The night was filled with noises, low grunts, low snorts. At his shoulder, Astrid was just passing her sword neatly through the throat of another wolf, the creature's death-howl cut off by sharp steel. At his back, Issar was kicking at one wolf trying to swarm up his horse's flank, whilst fending off another with his scimitar.

Astrid tugged her weapon free from the dead wolf's neck. Swallowed the rising bile in her own throat. Wheeled to see that Jaska was down, face down on the ground, two wolves worrying her, and with a wild yell Astrid bore down on them, sending both wolves scampering back down the hill, out of reach.

'They're falling back!' cried Issar. Astrid wanted to go to Jaska, but knew she couldn't, not yet, not if any of them were to live. She turned back to the others, saw Leif lolling in his saddle, Issar bleeding from his leg and pointing down the hill. 'See,' he said, 'they retreat. Perhaps they'll just . . . slink away?'

Astrid looked. The seven surviving wolves were huddled in a group on the edge of the trees, a murmur of noise rising from them. As she watched, the three largest darted away and began to circle the base of the hill, keeping an even distance between them. Two more were lying on their sides licking their wounds – one, a battered shoulder, the other, a shallow cut from Issar's scimitar. They would both be up soon, she decided. The other two had their heads together. It was all so strange . . .

'I fear these are no ordinary wolves,' said Leif, through gritted teeth.

'After I killed that werewolf, the one who seemed to be their leader, I thought we were just facing animals. But it's almost as if . . . as if they're *talking*,' Astrid said, and Leif nodded.

'Then they're Vargar,' he grunted. 'Wolves that talk – the sort that mix with witches. It explains why they're not afraid of flame.' He nodded to the two torches, guttering in the grass beside Jaska, now moaning under Issar's ministrations.

Astrid had a vivid memory of how she had met Leif, more than a year before, when he had fought off wolves with burning fire. He had repeated the trick later – but that time a witch had appeared . . . She blinked. 'So, they can talk. That doesn't change things much. We need to get out of here.' Her brows knit in thought. 'There are gaps in their circling. What if we all broke through in one place? We could outrun them, gallop off . . .'

Issar, looking up, shook his head. 'You forget that we've been riding all day – and now this. The horses are blown. We'd be caught in no time, and from behind. If anything, we're safest here, with these rocks at our backs. But the horses won't last much longer.' He glanced around. Grimaced. 'And neither will we.'

'They won't give up, since you slew their captain,' said Leif. 'The werewolf – I suppose he was Ormulf? Doubtless they will be thirsting for revenge.'

Astrid shot him an angry glance. 'Thanks for that,' she said. 'Next time I ride in and save you, I'll remember *not* to hurt the ravening monster.'

'I didn't mean –' Leif began, but Issar cut across them both. 'Look,' he said. They all turned back to the Vargar.

The four beasts were all standing, muzzles pointed up, ears quivering, looking at something above them. Then yet another piece of night peeled away from the sky. With a beat of heavy wings that set Leif's teeth on edge, an enormous black bird soared out of the void and landed on a branch beside their heads. Incredibly, rather than pouncing, the Vargar shrank back, bellies to the ground, ears flat. The three watchers strained to hear – the bird was definitely speaking – but the distance was too great.

'I don't know why we're not dead yet, Allah be praised, but if anyone feels like making themselves useful?' Issar had Jaska's head cradled in his arms, thick fingers lightly

46

smoothing down the black hair stuck with sweat and blood to the girl's forehead.

'How is she?' Astrid asked, the guilt at once a stone in her stomach.

'This child stands as much chance as any of us of lasting the night,' Issar said – and though his voice was gruff, his eyes were dancing with smiles – 'but if she's to make a full and fast recovery, she needs something for these cuts.'

'Perhaps,' said Leif, 'if I could say some words?'

A flapping from behind them and they wheeled back round, in time to see the great bird launch itself into the air. In another moment, it was gone from sight, melting back into black. The Vargar, too, were slipping away, back into the trees – all save one, the biggest. It padded slowly up the hill towards them, enormous paws, alert and yellow eyes.

It spoke.

'*Our master calls us off. One of you four is marked: somehow you displeased him. His is the right to hunt, and so we spare your lives. Soon comes the reckoning.*'

Its voice was a grey growl, the words feral. They had the wild still within them, and the listeners felt a howl was just below the surface of its speech. Astrid shivered. The Vargur went on.

'*Upon midsummer's morn, my master takes his prey. Till then, walk freely here; this forest will be safe. But you slew our brothers – beware. We are watching.*'

The final words slurred into a bark, and it half started forward – then, taming itself, the animal turned its back on them, and stalked into the trees.

None of them felt it was over. They knew that seven pairs of yellow eyes were watching from the darkness.

'What now?' said Jaska, after a long pause. They were the first words she had spoken, and though they were weak, nothing could have heartened the others more.

'Try to get some sleep, I suppose,' said Issar, laying a riding cloak over Jaska's shivering body. 'There's nothing else to do. Should someone stand watch?'

'I'll go first,' said Astrid at once.

'No need. The Vargar always keep their word,' said Leif.

'And how would you know? You mean, they keep their word in the stories you've learnt,' Astrid said.

Leif drew breath . . . let it go . . . nodded. Astrid paced the dreadful hilltop, winding her circuit away from where the dead Vargur lay. The others huddled down against the stones that did *not* have bloody pictures on.

No one slept.

†

'This is pointless,' said Issar, some time later. 'And if we can't sleep, we may as well talk. Make our plans.'

'Will we have to head back to Trelleborg?' said Jaska.

'No,' said Astrid. 'We go on.' She thought of the grey ship behind them, of that terrible man who had thrown the spear. They had to keep moving. 'On to Birka,' she said. 'We can all begin again there. Make new lives for ourselves, or' – she gestured to Jaska – 'go back to our old ones.' There was no going back for her, Astrid, she knew that much. 'And you heard what that wolf said. If he was speaking the truth –'

'He was,' said Leif.

'Then,' Astrid continued, 'we can travel freely in the forest until midsummer. That's nearly a moon away. Plenty of time.'

'If Jaska recovers,' Leif pointed out. 'She's our guide.'

'She will,' said Astrid. She kept her voice firm, and hard, as if she knew what she was talking about. It seemed to do the job.

Issar had been lost in thought. 'What the wolf said . . .' he mused. 'That first bit – we were all so surprised it spoke at all that we half missed what it was saying. At least I did. Something about their master – I thought Ormulf was their master? – and one of us displeasing him. Or was that bird their master?' He shook his head in confusion.

Leif opened his mouth. Astrid stood hard on his toes. 'Oh, I'm as lost as you are,' she said, speaking fast. 'Could be any of us. Probably me, actually – I killed two of them after all. As if I had a choice. Still, you can't expect justice from a bunch of talking wolves. Now, we really *must* try to sleep.'

But later, as Issar snored and Jaska snuffled, Astrid bent low to Leif's ear. 'That bird,' she whispered, 'was a raven.'

He nodded.

'One of Odin's ravens?'

He nodded again.

'Which means,' she hissed, 'that their master is Odin. Can we think of anyone here who's annoyed the king of the gods?'

49

'Well, thank you for not telling the others,' Leif whispered. He thought back to his argument with Odin's raven, as he lay on the point of death beside the Yelling Stones. How he had refused to help the old gods; had threatened the bird itself. His arrogance seemed to belong to another person. He felt none of that now. He was only tired. Very, very tired. But he forced his head around to look at Astrid.

'All the same, there's something not quite right here,' he said. 'Since when have the Vargar worshipped Odin? Since when have werewolves sacrificed to gods? This was never a part of the old faith – it's as if someone's changing the stories . . .'

Astrid shrugged. 'Does it really matter? It's not stories that can hurt us now – it's the real world.'

'I wonder,' he said, so softly that she almost missed it. 'And, Astrid, I'm trying to remember – I'm so tired it's making me stupid – all that about their master and his prey . . . what is it that happens at midsummer?'

'Search me,' she said.

'The Wild Hunt.' It was Jaska, half awake, paler than ever. Had she been listening?

'At midsummer in the North, when twilight lasts forever. It is then that Odin rides out, and death to all who cross his path, or who run too slowly. The Wild Hunt.'

CHAPTER SEVEN

Haralt Bluetooth's face wore that rarest thing – a smile – and Arinbjorn's flesh crept. Just what sort of man had he pledged his allegiance to? A strong ruler, yes, but . . .

'I have just been in counsel with our two remaining German bishops,' the king was saying, and Arinbjorn hastily stiffened to attention. Haralt went on. 'They inform me they have made great progress in spreading the Word of Christ in their towns. The bishops are preaching all sorts against the old ways, inventing horrors in pagan Sweden – men becoming wolves and butchering their fellows in the name of Odin, terrible blood-sacrifices at Uppsala – and the people believe it. Our townsfolk now take those across the sea to be blood-hungry savages. It bolsters their Christian faith – and their allegiance.'

'It sounds not unlike that trumped-up charge for which we condemned Grimnir,' said Arinbjorn, without thinking.

Haralt narrowed his eyes. 'We had every grounds to believe those accusations of child-murder,' he said.

Arinbjorn flushed at his mistake. 'Grimnir and Reginbrand are not back yet, anyway,' he said, changing tack. 'Either they have carried on to Birka as we wished, or they've killed each other in some godforsaken forest.'

Haralt's mouth twitched. 'Either suits me,' he said. 'As long as they deal with those little outlaws first. Though I'd be sorry not to see that sword again . . .'

'Sword?' said Arinbjorn.

'Oh, nothing,' the king said. 'Besides, we must turn to business. How is the building work proceeding?'

᛭

Grimnir sniffed at the strong sea breeze. 'If this wind holds fair,' he remarked, 'we will weather the western cape of Gotland, and put in at Ridanaes by dusk.'

'And how does that serve our purpose?' Reginbrand was tetchy. His stomach had not improved as the voyage continued. 'The children are hardly likely to have come this way. All haste for Birka, that was the idea, wasn't it?'

'We'll be there before them, book-botherer, never fear,' said Grimnir. 'But the crew could do with a rest, and we need fresh water. I thought you'd be glad to set foot on dry land.'

'True enough,' said Reginbrand, as another lurch of the ship jolted his insides. 'I don't suppose there's a church in Ridanaes?'

'No,' said Grimnir. 'Though the Allfather knows there will be, if you have your way . . . No; what they do have is the most succulent lamb in all the world of men.'

Reginbrand shot him a sly look. 'Lamb, you say, young and tender? More innocents to the slaughter, I suppose?'

Grimnir's face tightened. The priest's words had for once struck home. In his old life, as a servant of Odin, he had performed his rites half out of his mind on potions and strong drink. There were gaps in his memory. But – no, impossible. He was a killer, and proud of it. But of *children*? Angrily he stalked away from Reginbrand, to stare at the approaching headland. His right eye – the one that had been struck by Haralt – was still twitching.

↓

Eyes between tree trunks, eyes on their backs; yellow eyes at night at the edge of the firelight. After a few days, the travellers became used to the sensation, of ever-wakeful death a few paces away, watching, always watching, so that slowly they forgot the Vargar were there. And then one of them would catch the swish of a tail or the slope of a low grey back in the bracken, and remember.

But for all that, they were happy. Jaska had declared herself fit to walk by the morning, and ready to ride the day after. Now they kept up an even trot along endless forest paths, north, north, always north. The girl sang, a curious high chirruping like the language of birds, and indeed, the birds sang back. And it was Jaska who, when supplies ran low, was the first to brave the wolf-roamed treeline, and stray beyond the path.

Barefoot, she padded a little way into the forest, rejoicing in the soft springing under her heels, the roughness between her toes. She was looking for roots, mostly, and maybe – if she was lucky – edible mushrooms. The season was against her. Far too early, she knew, for the best – those delicate golden music-horns – but there might be others. Hedgehog mushrooms, pale and tender; stone mushrooms, young and firm . . . *there*, in the mulching shade of a spruce, a whole clump of them, whitish-grey, brown-topped. She reached down, plucking up a handful, streaming dirt, gathering them to the folds of her tunic. At the back, in the darkest place, a larger clump – one big growth, hard to make out – and she stooped for that one too. And snatched back her hand, as the mushroom moved. A trickle ran down her spine as she looked up, straight into the eyes of the watching wolf.

She had been about to grab at its paw.

Nothing to be done – she had a hunting knife, but would never draw it in time – so she froze. The Vargur froze. Time passed. She became aware of its breathing: ragged, uneven, deep. On the very edge of its self-control. It bared wicked yellow fangs, dripping with drool, huge red tongue lolling. Then the heavy jaws snapped shut on empty air. A blur of pelt, a rustle of leaves, and the wolf was gone.

The four of them grew bolder after that.

'Mushrooms?' said Astrid, cocking an eyebrow, once Jaska, breathless, had told them of her encounter and endured a round of hugs.

'They're safe to eat,' Jaska said, her face falling.

'I don't doubt you! And they look delicious,' said Astrid. 'But you're a Sami, aren't you? A Lapp, from up north. Aren't you meant to all be great hunters?'

'Mine were reindeer people,' said Jaska, quietly. 'But I can lay traps, yes.'

'So consider it a challenge,' Astrid said.

Every night after that, Jaska set up snares around their camp. There was always at least a brace of rabbits in the morning. Every stream yielded its fish to the quiet little girl with the high cheeks and clever hands. Before long, she had made her own bow, and began firing shafts of wood to hardened points for hunting arrows. Her clothes changed too, day by day, almost unnoticeably, as bits of forest took over from spun clothing, and soon she was a gliding shimmer of bark and leaves, fur and fir.

As they rode, they talked little, save of what was around them, and where they were going. The shifting face of the forest, the unending forest, as they rode into the North and into early summer. Scents of sap and resin. Glorious spans of branches overhead. The queer gnarling of tree trunks into nearly human faces. The smoothness of polished stones under a plashing waterfall.

They spoke too of Birka, and their hopes. The rock-bottom price at which Issar might buy amber, and this winter's pelts. Jaska's tales of a wild childhood on the high fells and the taiga forest, the life she would go back to. Astrid's thirst for fame and glory as a shield maiden in the service of the marauding Swedish kings.

They did *not* talk about their pasts. No one asked why the two youths were on the run from a nameless Danish dread, nor why an Arab trader had wound up here in Sweden. How a Sami girl had fallen prey to slavers. There was a sense that those pasts had been left behind, and it would be breaking some sort of spell to drag them out here, in the open, under the trees.

Only Leif tried to talk to Issar, to put right what he had said before about his father's name. But for all his way with words, he found himself tongue-tied, and Issar avoided the subject. Except for one night, when Issar answered with a question about Leif's mother.

'She . . . she died,' was all Leif could say.

And Issar was silent for a long time after that.

The next night, Issar sat by Leif again. 'My boy, would you like to hear a story?' he said.

Leif nodded, heart thumping. Was this the moment? But Issar spoke not of himself, but of his people and his homeland. Of the far south, of the immense and tideless sea that was a deeper blue and as true as that of the northern sky. Of the groves of orange trees, of nights scented with lemon and jasmine. Of fountains in marble courtyards, and the stinging sands of the desert, where devils danced among the dust.

There were stories enough here to last Leif a lifetime, and at night he forgot his own questions, and let himself be enchanted. They pitched their camp in glades and glens when they felt safest; slept around a fire and under the stars, backs against horses, heads upon knapsacks, swaddled in darkness. By the glow of a dancing fire, the smell of woodsmoke and the soft chirrup of frogs and night birds the only distraction, it was easy to get lost in a story of the hot, jewelled, unknowable south. And by day, as they rode, Leif cared only for the world around him. The heady greens, the rise and tumble of mighty trees and their sweet-smelling burdens. The gentle backs of hills, like giants' shoulders, over which they rode, and the merry surge of streams where they bathed, drank and crossed. There was beauty in plenty here. They all saw it, and they all shared it.

And so, slowly, they noticed a change. Almost by accident, they had become friends. Jaska voiced all their thoughts. 'I wish this ride could go on for the rest of our lives.'

'Except,' said Astrid, 'that at midsummer this Wild Hunt begins. And if we're still in the forest then, the rest of our lives might not be very long.'

No one answered her. But each of them squeezed their heels a little deeper into their horse's sides, without realising. The pace quickened.

ᚠ

It could not last. Nor did it. Somewhere in the mountains to the east of the great inland lake – you could smell the freshness borne on the westerly breeze, and more to the point when the breeze died in the ever-later dusk, there were a hundred midges aiming for your ankles where there had been ten before – about halfway to Birka, somewhere to the east of the lake, Leif and Astrid quarrelled.

They had fought before. Had shouted, sworn, hurled things at each other. It always came right in the end. This was worse. This time, they did none of those things.

Leif was riding alongside Jaska. 'Our path lies on the same route as the lake – running north-east all the way, is that right?' he said.

'More or less,' she said. 'For the next day or two, anyway, then the shore heads north and we veer away again. No more midges!'

'That isn't what I had in mind – I thought we could perhaps ride right along the lake,' Leif said, now raising his voice to take in the whole company. 'I hate to miss such a beautiful sight, when it's barely even out of our way.'

Jaska paused – which gave Astrid the chance to speak up. 'No,' she said. 'We can't afford the time it would take: *any* delay could mean still being in the forest at midsummer.'

'Oh come on – what do the rest of you think?' said Leif. 'I'm sure that we can spare a day or so.' He saw it in his mind – trees to the right, sand underfoot, a horizon of limitless blue stretching off to their left. Sun and water – the poems he might write!

'I said no,' said Astrid. 'I'm sorry.'

'And who made you the leader? No one's sworn an oath to serve you – I don't wear your gold,' said Leif. Unnatural heat prickled his forehead, but he couldn't back down now, not in front of the other two. And she *had* been taking command of late. There rose, unbidden, the sight of her face on the dread hilltop, remote and awful. Like her mother's, or like her brother Haralt's. The red-running sword. Not that he was embarrassed, of course, at being saved – again – by her actions, whilst he cowered on the ground. Oh no.

'Someone has to take charge,' said Astrid. 'And *don't* start talking about Iceland like you always do. They may have no kings, but they *do* have a law-speaker. I asked.' She too was getting a little hot. It was just like Leif to want to take in the scenery, when the Vargur's threat hung over them. Over *him*, in fact – it was him Odin hated, and he knew it! But he wouldn't admit it in front of the others. In front of Jaska. Not that she cared how much time he spent talking to the little Sami girl. Oh no.

Leif spoke without thinking. 'Supposing someone *does* have to take charge – what right have you to claim it should be you?' And straight away he wished he hadn't said it.

Astrid flushed beet red. She had every right: she was the daughter of Gorm the Old, greatest king in all the North! She was *born* to rule. And that birth right had been taken from her, when she had lied, claimed to be a murderer, to save *his* life – which he knew – and she couldn't even speak of her claim, of their past, in front of the others – which he knew too! She was struck dumb. But her face told of her anger.

Jaska put a hand on Leif's shoulder as they rode on. 'It doesn't matter anyway,' she murmured. 'You can't ride along the edge of the lake. It's all rocky.' She hesitated. 'Maybe I should have mentioned that a bit sooner . . .'

CHAPTER EIGHT

No one referred to the fight again, and the next morning, Astrid and Leif seemed all smiles. But to prove a point, Leif rode out early and ahead of the others at a smart trot. And, to prove a point, Astrid lagged behind the rest at a modest walk. And something shifted in the air around them. The trees unbent themselves, and reknit in different ways. No one noticed. But the forest had noticed the change in the travellers. The forest was awakening.

Leif rode into the most glorious morning he had ever known. Sweet scents wove about him, pollen, bracken, pine. With the sun came a wash of gentle birdsong: bramblings, warblers, fieldfares – skitters and chirrups – and a delicious warmth stole over his skin. Leif writhed with pleasure in his saddle. His right cheek was bathed in young light. The sun he knew in truth to be a woman, Sol, a chariot-rider, forever fleeing Skoell across the sky. Skoell was yet another wolf, and one day he would catch Sol, at the ending of the world. *But not today*, thought Leif. This was not a day to fall prey to wolves, and that cheered him, because when he thought of Sol, he saw, not a mighty charioteer, but Astrid. What in his world was more like the sun than her? Even if she burnt him sometimes . . .

He kicked in his heels, urging the horse on, as if he could outride the argument he had started. He was learning, catching the rhythm of the rising trot, making good use of those funny things that Issar called 'stirrups'. His body rose and fell with his breathing and with the breathing of his horse, sinews easing, muscles thrilling. The path was clear and dry, and when a little later Leif began to feel thirsty, he at once caught the sound of running water.

'Whoa,' he said, a gentle twitch on the reins. The way opened up into the bank of a broad stream, rushes to either side, bent necks of white willow, flashes and darts of colour as dragonflies zipped in and out of sight. On the far side, in the trees, a large form – not a wolf, but the lovely spots of a fallow deer. This must be a good place. The corner of his eye caught the scampering shape of a water vole, diving into undergrowth. A merry party of eider ducks ignored him, bobbing and bickering away to his left. And to his right on the far side, sun-dappled and indistinct as he squinted, there was – what, exactly?

Leif slipped from the saddle and let the horse edge nearer the bank, plunge its head, and drink great snorting draughts of cool clear water. Shading his eyes, he took a pace or two to the right. He wanted to get a good look at the . . . at the whatever-it-was.

Just a fallen birch, one slim branch dangled in the stream. A sapling – brought down by storms? – its fallen foliage, tangled in grasses, a rich deep brown, its bark silvered, its . . .

And Leif for once was lost for words, as the birch tree peeled itself free of the bank and stood, looking across at him. It smiled. With one slender hand it made as if to pin up the tumbled chestnut locks that spilled about its shoulders. She was beautiful.

There was a humming in Leif's head. He blinked. Some bees were flitting about a spill of yellow flowers close at hand. How had he taken her for a tree? He made to speak, to question her, and she raised a finger to her lips. A flicker of movement at her ankles, a soft brown wisp beneath the hem of her plain white dress.

He knew what she was then. That wisp was a tail, and she was a Huldra. A guardian of the forest, a tempter of youths.

A devourer of men.

His grandmother, a Finnish witch, had warned him of these northern spirits, creatures of tree and shade. Had warned him of their charming smiles that hid needle-sharp teeth, of an embrace as soft and ensnaring as that of snow.

Mind you, she'd also warned him that all Swedes had two heads and all Norwegians had forked tongues.

Even if it were true, he thought, unblinking – even if it were true, it might be worth it.

Her smile broadened. The stream between them was a mere nothing, a thread of blue wool – he could leap across it and be in her arms . . .

The water was a chill lapping at his ankles. When had he stepped into the stream? Leif's horse gave a loud neigh of what sounded like laughter and he blushed crimson.

The Huldra laughed too. 'Oh, silly boy, put away your blushes! I'm rarely in the way of stealing souls.'

Her voice was the sigh of zephyrs in the leaves.

Leif backed hastily out of the stream, trying to save face. 'Never would I make such a suggestion! Even if your under-shift *is* showing,' he said, with a cough. Taking his meaning, she whisked the tail out of sight beneath her dress. 'I thank you for your tact, young traveller,' she said. 'Few who walk the forest have such manners.'

'Manners are what I have in place of looks,' said Leif. He was beginning to enjoy himself. 'But the two are melded with skill in you.'

Her laugh was a ripple of blossom falling on a still pond. 'And now it seems that *I* am being lured,' she said. 'Well, silver tongue, this forest is your friend from here on in; on this you can depend. I hope that you will linger in it long.'

'Till midsummer. It turns against me then,' said Leif. 'The Wild Hunt will make quite sure of that – I need to be in Birka before then.'

'Well, curse the Allfather for a fool,' she said, eyes flashing wildfire. 'His haughty race make sport among our trees without a care for those who call it home. Every year the Wild Hunt rides forth – usually we spirits are its quarry. Death and grief brought to the quiet places; the spear-point turned on those who mean no harm!' She spat, a gob of green, resinous sap. 'A plague on gods who set themselves on high.' And she tossed her head, shedding scraps of twig and bark.

Leif grinned. She had a temper to match Astrid's, it seemed. He paused, caught between a memory of his friend and a need to say something, to keep this lovely person talking and bask awhile in her company. To his dismay, he saw her frown, shiver, start like a hare. The next instant she was gone, flitting between trees, merging with them. Was it something he had said? Or, no, rather something he had thought . . .

But in the same moment, he heard, as she must have done before him, the drumming of hoofs on baked earth. Leif sighed. To the empty air he said, 'I hope, in time, to speak with you again.'

As if in answer, a single birch leaf settled on his forehead. He caught it in his palm. Looked around. There were only beech and willows within reach. Leif smiled, tucking the leaf inside his tunic, and turned to greet the others.

ᛁ

Astrid made every effort that morning to defer to the others. When Hestur shied, a stone snagging the sole of his hoof, she stopped to see to the injury. If neglected, such a bruise could send a horse lame. 'I'll catch you up,' she called, waving them away down the track.

As she bent over Hestur's raised hoof, one hand stroking his quivering fetlock, the other exploring the hurt spot, Astrid began to feel uneasy. As if something were burning between her shoulder blades – the point where a spear or dagger could plunge in – and she knew then that she was being watched. Slowly, very slowly, she lowered Hestur's leg back to the ground. He would be fine. For a moment she squatted on her heels, eyes on the dusty, grass-peppered earth. Ants scurried across lichen, twigs, last year's leaves. Then she spun in a single movement, rising and turning and drawing her sword. Eyes blazing, blade outstretched, she found herself staring straight into the face of . . .

'A bird on a branch!' she said, half laughing, half annoyed at herself. But no: not just a bird. A raven.

It hunkered low in an ash tree, head on a level with hers, and – as it was on the eastern edge of the path – it wore a shroud of shadow. Even on a summer's morning, there was something of the night about it. Until you really looked at a raven, looked hard and close, you did not see it for what it was, she thought. Did not see the truth in the weight, the curve, the sharpness of its cruel talons, and its crueller beak. Leif, she knew, had plenty of names for ravens. Drinker of the dead sea. Hymir's skull-picker. Blood-bird of battle. And she wrinkled her nose, at once aware of a foul smell that had not been there before.

Wound-worrier, said the voice in her head; *strife-seeker*. And another name, that rose, insistent, to the front of her mind. *Hawk of Odin.*

'*Greetings, daughter of Gorm,*' it said. '*Good to see you so well.*'

Its voice was a rasping of charcoal, and it set Astrid's teeth on edge. 'Look,' she said, with more confidence than she felt, 'if you're going to talk in poems all morning, then I'll make you a new mouth to spout them from with this sword.'

'*Aha! A metaphor!*' it said. '*Astrid the skald, is it?*'

She frowned. 'That was poetry too,' she said. 'I warned you.' And she brought the Toledo blade a handspan nearer its throat. The raven hopped from leg to leg. '*Careful, would-be* shield maiden,' it said. '*The boy used threats against me and it angered my master.*'

'Leif annoyed Odin because he wouldn't kill Folkmar,' said Astrid, irritated. 'Don't puff yourself up, black sparrow. And now Folkmar's dead anyway. Can't Odin let it go? Just, I don't know, forgive and forget?'

The raven crowed with displeasure. '*You talk like a Christian, gold-haired girl. Revenge is the root of all order. The Allfather does not forgive. He sees justice done, on the point of his spear if need be.*'

'But you haven't come here just to throw empty words,' said Astrid. 'We know the Wild Hunt will ride against us come midsummer, the Vargur told us.'

'*Against the boy,*' the raven said. '*Not you. You are the daughter of a mighty king. You were born a hunter. That is why I am here.*'

Astrid felt a sudden chill around her ankles, as if her feet had been plunged into cold water. Looking down, she saw the raven's shadow, long and monstrous, swallowing the light about her feet. How could it be growing longer, when the sun was rising?

'*You were not born to run with these mongrels. You were not born to be prey.*' The raven spoke on into her silence. '*You seek to be a shield maiden, to serve in the war band of a Swedish king. Yet even that is a sorry fate for the brightest child of Gorm the Old. If you are to serve, you should serve a higher power.*'

The shadow was lapping at her shins now. Astrid took a step backwards. 'I really have no idea what you're on about,' she said. 'And I wish you'd go away. You're spoiling the sunshine.'

'*Then heed your destiny,*' said the raven, '*and dare to stand nearer the sun. To ride near Sol herself.*'

'Eh?'

'*You are chosen, Gorm's daughter. You have proven yourself in combat, upon witch and upon werewolf. Odin is well pleased. Such a mistress of the sword dance would well adorn the ranks of his Valkyries.*'

The breath caught in Astrid's mouth. 'Valkyries?'

'*He seeks no answer now,*' said the raven. '*The High One wishes only for you to know, that when the Hunt rides out, it is not your place to cower, but to join.* The Hunt does not come for you. *It is not your fate, when life is at an end, to go under the ground with the pale hosts of Hel, but to ride upon the storm, wield the weapon of judgement, choose between the slain . . .*'

'Stop!' she said, 'stop.' Half her body stood in darkness; the bird's harsh croaks were scraping through her head – and visions of the sky-ride were dancing in her eyes. She clutched at her forehead with her free hand.

'I have heard you out,' she said. 'Now let me be. I must catch up with my friends.'

'*Go with the speed of gods, Gorm's fairest-begotten,*' said the raven. And in an explosion of plumage, it was gone, a speck upon the sky.

One single feather, unnoticed by Astrid, settled on her shoulder. As she lowered her sword arm, it slipped beneath the hem of her tunic.

For years, it had been her greatest worry: what happened when you died. Had been the one thing above all others that had drawn her to Folkmar's faith – the promise of a heaven. The Danes had always believed that warriors, killed in battle, went to Asgard – and that women and children went with the thralls, to Hel, a dank, cold land under the earth. She had always hated small spaces, the dark and the dirt. To ride forever through the skies instead . . .

But what had the raven said, about hunters and hunted? What, that she should abandon her friends, turn against them even? It was unthinkable. And they would reach Birka days before midsummer, out of these old trees, into a life of promise and glory. Even if Leif did insist on dawdling. Although, if anyone was lagging behind that morning . . .

'Come on, Hestur, you old idler!' she said, and swung up into the saddle. The stallion neighed in indignation and excitement. She hardly had to touch her heels to his flanks; they were away, dust rising in their wake.

CHAPTER NINE

They had left the high places behind, ridden out of the hills and valleys, and now the slopes ran gently down and the trees all bore green leaves. Game was plentiful; there was always a stream for water and a lake to bathe in. Their evening campfires climbed into an empty sky. They saw no men, though the path being there at all was testament to the existence of other travellers. It was also used by deer and elk, and they rarely saw those either. Few animals lingered when sixteen hoof-beats tremored through the forest. But sometimes the red flash of a fox sent Leif's head swivelling, and he saw many signs of earths, setts, burrows.

Leif was finding within himself an endless store of love for almost all about him. This was a world without dead walls, where all was growth, life, expression. He said little, but stored away every detail. The tiny yellow-green catkins on the young-budding oaks, their splayed-finger branches mottled with lichens. The empty, hedgehoggy cases of last autumn's chestnuts. The ceaseless, shifting dapple of light and shade. They came upon a clearing, perhaps once devastated by a fire, now a haven of teeming flowers and a well of golden light. The whole forest floor was covered with white, thousand upon thousand of starflowers just peeking their soft white petals above coppered leaves. Leif blinked. It looked like snowfall. His eye travelled out, to the interlacing of twinflowers, frail white trumpets, and further still to the ferns at the clearing's edge, brimming over with lady's-slipper orchids. And then he all but fell off his horse – he had caught the outline of a slender leg, an arm, where he had thought there was only white birch, and above, wreathed in chestnut hair, a secret smile. His Huldra. Leif blinked. She was gone. But he wrapped up the memory, and stowed it away carefully near his heart.

Astrid saw his lingering, dreamy looks, and said nothing. She would not provoke another fight. But really, it was ridiculous. All they had planned, all they had dreamt, lay ahead, in Birka and beyond. *Iceland or anywhere*, she remembered. They had vowed to see the world, and Leif would soon grow tired of the forest – or it of him. He couldn't hunt, couldn't carve; all his art was made for men, and he needed people around him to work, to protect him. People like her. And for her part, Astrid had had quite enough of the forest. The scratches of holly and low-hanging branches as you rode by, the tug of an unseen spider's web dragging through your fast-growing hair, the endless caking of mud and dust that meant your legs and clothes were never quite clean. And it was so rarely that you ever saw the sky – *really* saw it, vast and blue, not hemmed in and crowded out by all these grasping trees . . .

Give me the open, she thought. *Give me the sea and the field of battle.*

Once, she yielded to her temper and spoke out. 'Leif, what would you *do* out here?'

'I would compose the poem of the wood,' he said, simply. But there was something in the way he spoke that she recognised: there was ambition here. Probably he had in mind one of those poems that took from one moon to the next in the telling.

'But, Leif,' she said, 'Leif – just who would you tell the poem *to*?' Because she knew that his hunger for glory, for fame, was as great as hers. But she did not know of his secret spirit in the trees. And he smiled, and gave her no answer.

'There is such a thing as winter, you know,' said Jaska to Leif. 'It isn't all sun and plump pigeons and easy riding.' But for all that, he still spent the ever-shorter evenings asking her about the wild life of the Sami, and Issar had to save his tales of Al-Andalus and the Arab courts for Astrid.

One evening, they rode up clear of the treeline, to pitch camp on a scrubby hilltop. By the light of a glorious sunset, Astrid, exultant in the openness of sky, began to inspect and polish her sword. Issar went quiet. It was the first time he had seen it clearly. 'That sword,' he said at last, in a murmur. 'Where did you get it?'

Astrid looked up. 'It was my father's,' she said, with an edge to her voice. Then she relaxed. 'Well, sort of – it was given to him – but my brother stole it, so I stole it from him.'

'Oh,' said Issar. The code of respect that had grown up among them prevented him asking any more.

'It was Leif's father's before that,' said Astrid, sensing his curiosity. 'He left it to Leif's mother, or something like that. It's a long story.'

Issar let out a long sigh. Muttered something that could have been 'so she kept it' or 'no more like it' or even 'hone and whet it', for all Astrid could make out. Well, he was a trader; it was a valuable blade – from his part of the world, too. She frowned, meaning to speak, and then Jaska snuggled down between them. 'It's a beautiful sunset,' she said. 'When I look at that, Issar, I can almost believe in that paradise of yours.'

And that sent Astrid's thoughts off in another direction, and later, nestled into a heathery cleft of rock, face open to the sky, she had a dream.

þ

She was flying.

Never before had Astrid flown in a dream. Danced, yes, skied, yes, died – twice – in a horribly vivid dream she'd had on two occasions, years apart, when she'd been closed up in a cave under the ground. Since that had actually happened to her, last winter, the dream had not returned . . .

But never *flown*. And here she was, treading the great arc of dawn and dusk across the world's rim. Below were the clouds, behind was the sun, and the rush of air sent her hair streaming like a banner, for her hair was long again in the dream.

She knew what was going on. That she would wake. But it didn't make it less real, just worth savouring all the more, in the knowledge that, soon, it would end.

'What if it didn't?' said a voice.

Startled, she spun right round – the easiest thing in the world now she was light as a single swan's feather – but she was alone.

'Didn't what?' she said anyway, to the air.

'Didn't end,' said the voice. It was like her father's voice, but more so – a hundred times more so – high, haughty, but honeyed; there was power there, and frailty, and above all it was old – old, old, old . . .

'Everything ends,' she said, only half her mind on the conversation. She *knew* that voice, or had known it before.

And without noticing how, Astrid found she was riding – still flying, but riding – and it was her own dear Hestur beneath her, galloping through dizzyingly thin air.

'That horse of yours,' said the voice. 'How old is he?'

Astrid opened her mouth to answer – and closed it again. She understood.

'You don't have to lose him,' it said. 'Neither of you would age.'

She had the sense that another horse was beside her – behind, above, *somewhere* near – massive, strong, fast as the wind. She almost heard the pounding of eight mighty hoofs. Felt the chill of its ancient shadow. And she knew who its rider must be. If she turned, fast, to look over her shoulder, she would see – would catch a glimpse – *him* . . .

And she dared, she did it, and there was a face, saying her name; but it was Leif's face, and she was lying wedged into a cold rock on a bare hillside and she glared at Leif with such venom that he flinched, and turned away to where the others were already saddling the horses, and Hestur was earthbound, lovely, and looking less than young.

⚡

'So,' said Issar, 'has anyone here actually *been* to Birka?'

'I have,' said Jaska, after a moment's silence. 'You know there are actually two parts to Birka, two settlements? Birka itself, where the markets and the people are, is on one island, and the kings' hall, Hovgarden, is on a larger island just to the north. You'd probably want to split up . . .' She tailed off into her own thoughts, as Issar shot a thoughtful look at Leif: clearly, their different aims led to two different islands.

Jaska shuddered as her memories of Birka thronged around her. She had been so young – six or seven – when some of her tribe had come to the Swedish capital to sell their furs, pelts and reindeer jewellery. She had found Birka a terrifying place, where unfettered trees gave way to walls, walls, walls – wooden walls all about, so many gates, the high fort glowering over the town, spreading its lifeless shadow . . . Even the ships, scudding free as birds on the river, were penned and hemmed into the little harbour by a seawall of timber. The houses, each like the other, small and squat, set out in exact lines, the little fenced-in patches of earth that passed for gardens – *gardens*, indeed, when outside the walls was a world of living forest. And the *people*! She had been spun and buffeted, left lost and bewildered in a crowd of hundreds, smelling rank with smoke or sweat or money. A tangle of unknown tongues, like being caught in a strange and sticky web – Slavs and Arabs

74

and Germans and Franks – and a tiny Sami girl lost and alone at the centre of that web. Where her people, her family, had gone, she never discovered. It was Ginnarr that had found her. To him, Jaska had been an investment – runner, skivvy, burglar if need be. In the years that had passed since then, half her life, Jaska had seen much of the world, and come to find that cruelty and discomfort were as much part of the open waves and the boundless horizon as they were of the cramped, smoky town and the walled-in marketplace. But that first panic of abandonment had stayed with her, left its mark.

'I can't go back,' she said, aloud. 'I'm not going back to Birka.'

Leif stared at her. Issar stretched out a hand in an imploring gesture.

'I'll take you there,' she said, her tone final. 'But I will not enter. Then I go on. On into the North.'

ᚠ

Two days later, they were there. Their weary mounts rested on a gently sloping shore. At their backs, pines, birch, spreading oak. At their shoulders, the high-hanging summer sun, nearly at its absolute zenith. And before them, the tranquil waters of the great lake, that wound down by broad and languid channels to the whale-roads of traders and Vikings. Sunlight danced across its surface, a brilliant sheen of blue and burnished gold. A cluster of islands lay in the lake, gigantic pebbles cast from on high to lie, scattered, grassy, tree-strewn.

'Where first?' said Jaska. 'Birka or Hovgarden?'

'Not to mention *how*,' said Issar.

For answer, Astrid pointed across the water, to where several boats – and even ships – were crawling, ant-like, over its surface. The light was exceptionally clear, and they could all make out the southern end of the sheltered harbour of Birka, shimmering with heat and teeming with craft. Away to the left was a low-lying island, the royal complex just visible in the distance: a squat burial mound (*Nothing like so grand as father's*, thought Astrid) and a great wooden hall. As they watched, that shore grew thick with what must have been people, milling and running, and soon, a low-riding, broad-bottomed ship cast off, at once lost to sight behind a smaller island between them and it.

'Our welcome party, I suppose,' said Astrid. 'We're four riders, on good horses – not those tubby ponies that pass for horses here in Sweden –' and she patted Hestur's neck in praise – 'it stands to reason that we need looking into. They'll take us to the kings. Well, that suits me,' she said, 'and Leif, and it can't hurt your prospects of business, Issar, if we make a good impression. Sorry, Jaska,' she finished up, 'but at least you won't be going to Birka. And there's sure to be a good feast to set you on your way.'

Issar narrowed his eyes. 'You seem very confident that a few ragtail runaways and wanderers will find favour at a royal court, Astrid. It's always been my experience that we commoners and outcasts never fare well when our rulers take too close an interest in us.'

Leif jumped in. 'Ever the optimist, that's our Astrid,' he said. 'Besides, we have learning, words and some wealth

– there's no reason to be bashful here.'

'How about a last meal, while we wait?' said Jaska. Whilst they had been talking, she had unbent her bow into a fishing rod, and in moments, felt the first twitching of the line. Before long, several perch were spitted and turning over a small fire.

'How does she do it?' Issar shook his head in wonder.

It was a glorious meal in every way. For once, repelled by the sweet-smelling fire, the insects left them in peace, and the four travellers, so soon to part, savoured each other's company. They sat, backs warming in the sun, on the lake's edge, and talked of very little. The perch were delicious, fresh and charred, flavoured with herbs from the bank and the forest edge. The lightest of breezes played about their faces. Jaska sang a quiet, sad song, half under her breath, half ringing clear, that she called a 'yoik'. None of the others could make out any real words, a structure, or even much of a tune, but in the thin, lilting sound they heard the world around them as if distilled, intensified: open water and sheltering trees, something ending, something starting.

Issar surprised Leif by suggesting that they take themselves a little way off to bathe, splashing about in the shockingly cold water. Each was struck by a likeness in the face of the other, the hard lines of jaw and nose, the jet black of their hair, something around the eyes. And in the end, both were smiling, despite the cold. Neither spoke as they basked themselves dry, but as they walked back to the others, Issar finally laid a hand on Leif's shoulder. And then both of them began at once. 'It seems that we are soon to part,' said Issar, as Leif blurted out, 'I am not ashamed of my father's name.'

Issar grimaced, held up a hand, took a deep breath. 'I . . . I've something to tell you,' he said. 'Tonight.'

'Why not now?' Leif's voice was quiet, hushed. Half afraid, and half hungry.

'Because before I can tell you, boy, I need a drink.'

'I thought your faith did not allow liquor,' Leif said.

'It doesn't. But it would take the nerve of the Prophet to get through the conversation without one,' said Issar.

'Tonight, then,' Leif said. There were goosebumps on his warming skin, and a glow of anxious anticipation in his belly. And from the other side of the dune came Astrid's rich, ringing laugh, and in a moment, they were back with the others.

'That ship's taking forever to arrive,' said Astrid. 'They must have landed north of here – somewhere sandier, perhaps, more forgiving on the hull. I thought we might ride up to meet them.'

'No reason not to. Let's be on our way.' For once, Leif agreed with Astrid. He was no longer so sure that all he wanted lay in Birka, or in Hovgarden – but the forest would wait for him, after all. More than anything, he needed to get Issar a drink.

'I can hear them coming anyway,' said Jaska a moment later, as they were saddling up. As usual, she was alone in this, her hearing so much more acute in the wild places. Jaska could pick out the drone of a bee beside a waterfall; could hear a snake glide over the noise of a woodpecker's knocking.

But then they all heard, and the thunder came upon them, a galloping horse-borne storm of fury, and the great grey man from the mad night in Hedeby led the charge, his huntsman's howl piercing the summer's day.

CHAPTER TEN

The storm broke in iron and men, dust and shouts. 'Away!' screamed Astrid, leaping onto Hestur. Her eyes were maddened, darting in every direction, her face a mask of terror and resolve. Cantering past Jaska, she hauled the girl bodily onto her mount, thwacking its flank with her scabbarded sword to send it on its way. This was no time to draw, to fight.

Huge, heavy men, tall horses, rank sweat and greased metal. 'Take the girl alive,' someone was shouting. 'The blonde one.'

Confused, Issar was still struggling, feet missing stirrups, straps twisting and knocking.

Leif was up and seated, but he was nearest the pursuit. 'Go like the autumn gale, gallant swift-galloper,' he whispered in his horse's ear. Far from his best – he was breathless and afraid – but the animal shot forward, whisking beyond Issar.

Turning in the saddle, Leif saw, out ahead of their pursuers, the grey spearman of Hedeby. His ear throbbed with the memory of that meeting, and his stomach turned as he saw the man had that spear again in his hand, and now he stood in his stirrups, seeking his balance, hefting the wicked shaft.

For an instant, their eyes met, and Leif knew the spear was marked for him.

Blood-snake. Illness of Odin. Blood-candle. Kennings for the weapon flickered through Leif's mind. *Corpse-lightning. War-needle.* None came near the hateful truth, he thought, of living wood shaped and spoiled, the better to kill.

Leif swung back, ducked in his head, tugged sharply on the right rein to jerk his horse aside, desperately trying to throw off the killer's aim. So no one saw the man hurl the spear, saw Issar, bellowing like a stuck bull, hurl himself sideways from his saddle, taking the silvered point in the centre of his chest – no one saw the big, burly man fall, transfixed, dead.

Grimnir rode over Issar's spitted body, rode through the still-smouldering fire where the perch had roasted. 'On! On!' he screamed, his good left eye blazing. He could fashion another spear when this hunt was done. What mattered was the chase, the finish; the price of his freedom and the lifting of the lie that tainted his name. He would do it with his teeth if need be. Behind him rode eight more, Reginbrand among them.

Astrid had to check Hestur to keep him from outstripping Jaska's little mare. The panicked horses surged through the trees, all paths abandoned, trampling ferns and brambles, thorns raking their sides and the girls' ankles. 'Where can we go?' said Astrid, between ragged pants.

'That little lake, a while back, up the hill,' said Jaska. 'If we can outstrip them, keep out of sight, we can . . .' She retched, gasped, breathed slow. 'We can canter through the shallows. The far side's . . . all rocky . . . we'll leave no hoof-prints. Shake them off.'

Astrid nodded. And they probably could, she thought, outstrip them – the men were heavier, they had weapons, armour; their horses might be fresh and ready for the long haul, but would never match animals ridden by women and a boy over a short sprint . . . though what about Issar? He would just have to make it – she couldn't solve everything – the din was rising behind them, whoops and snorts and clashing of metal on metal – where the *Hel* had they come from? Why hadn't she seen them? But they *had* seen them, the low-laden ship – the huntsman from Hedeby – they had sailed straight here! She shook her head in disgust. It had never occurred to her that Haralt would have the nerve to send men to the Swedish court itself. Here, she had thought, they would be free.

She came fully to her senses as Hestur swerved past a gnarled and crippled oak, nearly dashing her brains out on a branch. And then they were clear of the trees again and coursing up the hill, horses blowing hard. Turning, she saw Leif a few lengths behind her, barely clinging to his panicked horse but somehow clearing the trees in his turn, and she motioned him on. Together the three of them hurtled, skittering on loose shale, down the far side of the hill, the slope hiding them from the chase still crashing through the undergrowth behind them. Together, they drove the horses knee-deep into the cool water, thrashing up stillness into frothing white, led them to easy going in the shallows, jumped the telltale clay on the south side, clattered down onto smooth rock, vanished into close-crowding pines beyond.

Astrid urged them on at a trot, then hung back in the shadows near the trees' edge, squinting out from beneath dark green boughs into the bright sun that burnished the now-still lake. She saw the first rider crest the hill and pull up short, a brawny arm shading his eyes, scanning the lakeshore. Saw him throw both arms up to the skies in anger, saw the smear of red on his horse's fetlocks. Astrid knew what that blood meant well enough, and, heartsick, she turned, whisking away into the forest.

As she ducked beneath the branches, a yew-twig scraped across her back, and she shrugged her shoulders in irritation. A single black feather snagged free of her tunic and floated, lazy and unseen, to the ground, just clear of the trees. Its barbs, iridescent, caught the afternoon sun. Its shaft, long and pointed, lay towards the woods, where Hestur's faint hoof-print was half-formed in a bed of moss.

Astrid, shaking with unstoppered tension now the most immediate danger had passed, caught the others as they trotted through sprays of late-flowering hawthorn and springy young birch. Seeing her come up, unharmed, riding easily, the deathly hush lifted from the other two, so that Leif, turning first to the one and then the other, felt able to say, at last, without fear of blowing their cover: 'Where's Issar?'

ᚱ

The sun hung long in the sky; long enough to catch the fallen feather and make it shimmer in the light.

Reginbrand's eyebrows rose. For some time now he had watched, aloof, as Grimnir went over every handspan of ground around the lake, dropping to his hands and knees, sniffing the wind, prodding with twigs at sand and stone. He himself remained in the saddle, lordly on the brow of the hill – and well out of Grimnir's way. If he accidentally spoilt the traces of their quarry, there was no knowing what that madman might do . . .

Still, he'd better find something soon. Reginbrand was itching to return to Birka, to begin work on the new church the kings had let him found on the site of Unni's holy tomb. And then, back to Hamburg – by land, if possible – to take the credit in time for the next appointment to the archbishopric there. He could forget Sweden; even forget his wretched little position at Aarhus. If only Grimnir would hurry up.

And now the great grey Dane let out what was almost a bark of excitement, scrabbling, beast-like, on all fours to the edge of the trees. Triumphant, he rose, turning to Reginbrand, waving aloft . . . a feather.

'A feather?' The cleric curled his lip, but urged his horse down the slope nonetheless.

'A *raven* feather. It's a sign,' said Grimnir.

'Ah,' said Reginbrand, speaking each word very slowly, as if to an infant. 'A *raven* feather. Well, that's different. Because our task is, of course, to brave uncharted forests and untameable seas in order to catch for King Haralt . . . a raven. Oh no, my mistake – it isn't. That guilty conscience has finally pushed you over the edge, Grimnir.'

'The raven,' said Grimnir, all but snarling in his eagerness, 'is the sacred bird of –'

'Yes, yes, I know, of that demon you call Woden or Odin or whatever it is. It's still just a bird.'

'And did a bird make *that*?' said Grimnir, pointing to a patch of moss beneath the nearest tree.

'Our lord God made that. It's some moss.' Reginbrand was enjoying himself, but still . . . He wondered just how far this barbarian could be pushed before he snapped.

Grimnir smiled. 'It's a hoof-print, bookworm. I've found the trail.' He turned to address the men, who lay on the bank, eating and gambling. 'To horse, boys! The hunt is on!'

As they picked their way through the trees, pursuing the ever-clearer signs of their prey, Grimnir turned to Reginbrand. 'So, bishop, why is it that you worry me to death over these crimes I'm supposed to have committed? I'm not saying I did –' and his good left eye flashed wildly – 'but you scarce turn a hair over that big man I brought down earlier. He was an innocent, wasn't he? We had no cause to kill him.'

Reginbrand laughed. 'Innocent? Why, did you *see* the man? That wasn't an innocent, Grimnir, that was a Muslim.'

Grimnir spat, turned his gaze back to the trail. 'Sometimes I forget, Christ-man, that you're twice as ruthless as I am.'

☦

'I would have the forests burn for his pyre,' said Leif. 'I would string his killers from the gibbet, and have the gallows-birds feast on their eyes.' But the words rang hollow, even to him, and he lapsed again into silence.

They had all wept. Jaska was still sobbing, quietly, as she rode at the head of the three – only three – forever rubbing away tears that streaked her vision, as she tried to make out their bearing by the moss on the tree trunks and the fall of the foliage.

'He died beneath the trees,' Jaska managed to say. 'His spirit will be at peace.'

'He died in battle,' said Astrid. 'He'll have a place in Valhalla.'

'He died,' said Leif. '*He died.*'

†

The last embers of a scattered fire glowed lower, lower, under a dimming sky. The waters of the lake were darker now, the kicked-up dust long since settled. Unseen and unremembered, a lone horse, saddled and bridled, picked its way out of the birch wood, onto the bank. The coming night would be cold, and it sought the rider whose kind if heavy body had warmed it whilst it slept. Gingerly, it walked to his side, avoiding the cooling pool of red that spread beneath him and would cause its hoofs to slip. Bending its long, lovely head, the horse nuzzled at the rigid face, where the corners of the mouth still turned upwards in a grim smile. The face was cold, the man stirred not, and the horse turned away. There were bad things in the forest, and they would come for the man, drawn to the scent that hung like a disease in the horse's own nostrils. It would not do to be near when that happened, when the bad things came. A little urgent now, the horse trotted off. And night, as ever, fell.

CHAPTER ELEVEN

Once it was fully dark, the three fugitives took shelter in a thicket of hawthorn, dismounting and driving their horses through in spite of cuts and scratches. A fire was out of the question, but huddled so close, people and animals, all were warm. Warm, tired and hungry.

'Even if they've picked up our trail,' said Jaska, 'which will have taken them time, they'll have to stop for the night. You couldn't track even a herd of reindeer in the dark. A shame it grows light so soon: the horses could do with a real rest.'

Astrid shook her head. 'No chance,' she said. 'We have to keep moving, at first light. If they've followed us from Hedeby to Birka, they won't give up now.'

'All the way from Hedeby?' said Jaska. 'Then who are they? I thought Captain Ginnarr must have hired them.'

Astrid shook her head. 'I'm sorry,' she said. 'I'm sorry. But we've seen them before. That big grey man –'

'The one who –' Jaska began, then bit her tongue.

'Yes,' said Astrid, 'the one who killed Issar. I'd know him anywhere. We barely escaped him before. But I never thought they'd come so far – to an enemy court, to the wild . . .'

'Who is he?' said Jaska.

Astrid shrugged her shoulders. 'But I know who sent him.' She sighed, feeling the weight of it on her shoulders, in her chest – the guilt, the pain, the responsibility. 'My brother,' she said at last. 'My brother Haralt Bluetooth. King of the Danes.'

She had almost forgotten that Jaska was an outlander, a stranger, unfamiliar with her family and its story. 'Leif and I were falsely accused; outlawed,' she said. 'We tried to leave, but . . .' She shook her head. This wasn't the way to tell it. Leif would know how. But Leif wasn't talking.

'But why hunt you?' said Jaska.

'Haralt thinks we stole something of his.'

'What?'

'This sword.'

There was a pause. 'Well, you did,' said Jaska at last.

'It wasn't his,' said Astrid, flushing. 'Not really. He took it from our father's grave. It comes from the far south. Leif gave it to King Gorm, my father, in return for a job. Before that, it was Leif's father's.'

'Leif's father?' said Jaska. Now that the secrets of the past were tumbling out, she wanted more. It beat thinking about the present, anyway.

Astrid glanced over at Leif, hunched over and shivering. He was taking it very hard. 'Leif never knew his father,' she said. 'All he knows is that he was an Arab trader who passed through Hedeby about sixteen years a— Oh *no*!'

'I think he was going to tell me tonight,' said Leif. 'Once we had dined and drunk in Hovgarden. I cannot be entirely certain; I'd always thought his name was Ibrahim. But yes: I think Issar was my father.' And then he stood up, and pushed out through the thicket, and retched again and again.

|

The first birdsong brought them to their feet, stiff, cold and famished, and soon they were away at a nervous trot. The shock of Issar's death and the relentlessness of their pursuit had stunned them all, and there was only one thought in any of their minds: how they might escape.

'Are you *sure* you won't leave us?' Astrid asked Jaska. After all, the hunters weren't after her.

'My tribe could be anywhere across the North,' said Jaska. 'A moon's riding away. More. I'd thought I could ask someone in Birka for news. And even if we did split now, who's to say they'd follow your tracks, not mine? Or simply halve their forces? Better we stay together.'

'Then where do we head?' said Astrid. She had dreamt of the sky-ride again, had almost glimpsed the other rider. Her blood, her heart, was calling for revenge, for an end. But . . . 'We can't fight,' she said.

'We could,' said Leif. It was the first time he had spoken since he had been so violently sick.

'Leif, we've one sword and one bow between us. I'm sure Jaska and I could take a couple, but we're hardly the Varangian guard,' said Astrid. She was trying to be kind, to be gentle, but really – the things he said . . .

'There are other weapons,' he said, voice grim. 'You know the power that lies in well-picked words. And you yourself can summon forth a storm!'

'I've seen you start fires; turn swords to shrubs. And you said you bound Folkmar in his own church, that you overcame his angel,' said Astrid. Jaska stared in astonishment. 'But that was at Jelling,' Astrid went on. 'You told me yourself, your magic was a hundred times stronger there – all those years of worship around the stones, all that belief, making it a place of power.

'*But,*' she went on, forcing her point home, 'there's nowhere like that here in Sweden. Nowhere for us to make a stand, much as I'd love to.'

'There's the Great Temple,' said Jaska, so softly they almost missed it.

'The what?'

'The Great Temple at Uppsala,' she said. 'Even my people, who have no time for these high and mighty gods of your faith, show respect for the Great Temple. I can remember hearing the stories from my earliest days.' Jaska took a breath. She wasn't used to speaking at such length. 'There are no stones there. But there are burial mounds. They hold the power of the earth. There's the great tree. That holds the power of the forest. The sacred spring holds the power of the waters. And there's the temple itself. There lies the power of men. It is the holiest place the Swedes have. The great festival for the start of summer will be over, so it should be deserted. But all the potency, from the rites – that can't have just drained away, can it? If you really can tap the powers of belief, then that's the place to go. And it lies maybe nine days' ride north. I'm sure I can find us a way.'

Leif's face was hard as flint. There was hope. Not that he cared so much for their escape at that moment. But hope for revenge. For showing Issar, wherever he was, that Leif was sorry, and that he could be worthy.

Jaska's face gave little away. She was worried that she might lack the skill to lead them to the temple ahead of the hunters. But it was a plan; it was *her* plan, and it was well worth trying.

Astrid's face was shining. But then, Astrid's face was almost always shining.

'Uppsala,' they said.

'But first,' said Jaska, 'we will need to win time to shelter for more than one of these short nights, or else the horses won't make it. Be on the lookout for caves, tunnels, cracks in the hillside, that sort of thing. And I'll try to double back every so often and sweep our trail. We may as well *try* to throw them off, or at least make them waste time searching.'

They rode on. Astrid felt Jaska had rather spoilt the beauty of the moment with her common sense. Under her breath, she savoured the word once more. To her, it sounded like glory. Like the final stand of noble warriors. 'Uppsala,' she said.

†

Haralt Bluetooth was all smiles as he stood atop the earthworks at Fyrkat, surveying the progress of his first new fortress. It was immense, nothing like it in the North, and shaped as a perfect circle. Haralt's first mark upon his land. 'Bishop Leofdag has written a book,' he said.

Arinbjorn, hot, grimy and harassed from directing the labour of more than a hundred men, tried to look interested. 'A book, my liege?' His nails were filthy and broken, and it would take an age to comb the dirt and wood shavings from his grizzled, grey beard.

'Yes,' said Haralt, his lordly face serene. 'He intends to send it to Bremen, where there is talk of compiling a history of the Church in the North. It will be of great importance in securing my kingdom's place in Christendom. Leofdag writes such dreadful things of what they do in Sweden that, even if the Swedes convert, it will be clear that we Danes should rule in the North.' Haralt leered, showing his blue-slashed teeth. Below, men scurried in every direction, hauling fresh-hewn planks.

Arinbjorn winced. 'How so, Your Majesty?'

'Remember those sermons he preached about pagan sacrifice? About werewolves in Sweden?' Haralt laughed. 'Well, just wait till you hear what he has to say about the Great Temple at Uppsala!'

ᚼ

Reginbrand was uneasy. He had thought himself a strong man, but the riding was relentless. He had thought this mission simple, but the quarry was elusive. He had thought his authority secure, had thought Grimnir little more than his prisoner, but that grey savage had a way with the men that he lacked, always sharing their meals, jokes, hardships. He, Reginbrand, held himself apart, as a bishop and a leader should. But he could see it was losing him control over Haralt's warriors. Two or three had been Christians for years. But more were Danes, pagans till a year ago – less – and they kept slipping back into the old ways. This priest of Odin knew them better than he did. If ever things came to a head and he had to give the order, to kill or confine Grimnir . . . would they follow him?

'Come on, bishop!' called Grimnir. 'I've found their tracks again! It wouldn't do for you to be left behind – we're not the only nasty things in this forest.' And already, the others were past him, big men on big horses. Norsemen. Reginbrand mopped his brow, slapped at a midge, leaving a thin smear of blood on his exposed wrist. 'God forgive me,' he muttered, 'but I really, really hate Sweden.'

↑

By a placid stream, banked with sun-baked stone, an otter was worrying the remains of a fish. Between attacks on the rich white flesh, the otter would flip over on its back, rubbing itself against the stone, glorying in the heat like a cat by a hearth. All at once, the otter whipped upright, balancing on its hind paws, ears straight, wide snout twitching. Then it was off, abandoning its catch, slipping into the cool waters and away downstream. A moment later, three horses cantered into view, hoofs clattering on dry rock.

'Into the stream and up it!' cried Jaska.

'Can't we stop? Maybe water the horses?' called back Leif, lolling a little sideways in his saddle.

'No time,' said Astrid. 'Later. We can't rest without throwing the hunters off.' But she knew that even Hestur, her lovely, unstoppable Hestur, was near breaking point, and she herself not far behind, her stomach a knot of cramps, her thighs a living bruise.

'And not a hope of finding a nice cave,' muttered Leif. 'I thought Sweden was all hills and mountains, but it's as flat as Friesland around here.'

And they were gone, churning the crystal waters muddy, surging up the stream. It was some time before the otter returned to its meal. Not long after that, it froze again. Again, with a furious whickering, it melted away. Only just in time. A second thunder of horses was approaching.

CHAPTER TWELVE

'We can't stop here.' Jaska pursed her lips. 'Not enough cover.' They had dismounted by a brook in a wide glade, to let the spent horses slake their thirst. Even so, it didn't feel like resting. They couldn't get those spears out of their heads.

'*They've* stopped,' said Leif, gesturing behind them, to where a spiral of smoke, a greater dimness on a dim and twilit sky, showed above the trees.

'It could be a ruse,' said Astrid. 'Start a fire and keep on tracking, even in the gloaming. There's still a little light.' She herself was desperate for sleep. But not, she was quite certain, for a sleep everlasting.

'I swear there's something we're forgetting,' said Jaska, but at the same moment Astrid spoke over her. 'Leif,' she said, 'I know there's no power here, as such, but isn't there even a very little magic you could do? Spin spiderwebs across our trail, knit the trees together . . . ?'

Leif spread his hands. 'I've tried. But somehow I can't find the words. I'm all dried up inside, all emptiness.'

'I'm sorry,' said Astrid, biting down on the kernel of frustration within her. 'I know you're still grieving. We all are.'

'Some of us have more to mourn than others,' he said, almost too quietly for her to hear.

She went to him then, meaning to put an arm around his shoulders. 'I've lost my father too, remember?' she said. 'If I could make it better . . .' And she trailed off. A distance yawed between them. Both remembered, just as both remembered what Leif had once done, forfeiting glory and a triumph over Folkmar to make her feel better. If only she could do as much for him.

But she couldn't.

Leif really did feel hollow. Dry. Spent. He loved this forest; felt he knew it. Why could he not conjure up a poem, then, to turn it to his will? Angry at himself and Astrid, he stalked off through the trees. Out of sight and earshot of the others, he groaned, slump-shouldered, kicking a stray stone into a spinney of young birches.

A flash of russet, a wisp of movement. A fox?

He thought he saw a tail.

And just as he became aware of a gaze upon him, a voice spoke from the shadows.

'Beware, my southern boy, when kicking stones. You never know on whom your wrath may fall.'

It was his Huldra's voice. Leif whetted his lips with his tongue. Swallowed once, twice. The dryness in his innards was dissolving. 'Forgive me, lady. I was like the rain, not caring whom my sorrow fell upon. In this case I can see that my burden has beset the fairest flower of this forest . . .'

He gave up, out of practice and ideas. 'But may I ask what you are doing here? And grant that I may look upon your face?' He longed above all else to see that willowy form, that lovely face.

'Like ill fortune, I follow your travels,' she said, 'remembering that I promised you luck. It seems that I have been of little use. But time is short, and you need some shelter.'

Leif nodded, the all too real danger they were in forcing itself, unwelcome, on his mind.

'A short ride to the west, there lies a cave,' came the voice. 'Its occupant is elsewhere, as we speak. With luck, he may not seek his bed this night – at any rate, it is your only hope. Look for a rise of ground, a blasted stump. The entrance lies behind a screen of ferns.'

'My thanks – of course – but why is there no time?' said Leif. 'And why is it you will not show your face?'

'No time – must hide – poor boy, *it is tonight*!' There was a rustle, a tiny snap, and Leif opened his mouth – then closed it again. She was gone.

He shook his head, cleared the fog of his thoughts. '*No time*,' she had said. Well, that was true enough. He ran back to the others.

ƀ

Seven men lay sleeping on the ground, nine horses too, around a fire. The men's chests were barrels, bound with hard muscle, and they shuddered in and out as they snored.

Two alone were awake, hunkered down on either side of the fitful flames, wood smoke and cinders between them, the crackle of dry wood burning in their ears.

'Can't sleep, Christ-man?' said Grimnir. 'The forest floor too hard a bed?'

'How's your eye?' Reginbrand shot back, and Grimnir scowled. Whether it was infection, or something else, Grimnir had all but lost the sight of his right eye. His *eye*! They'd have caught the prey by now if he'd had both his eyes. Best in the North, his eyes had been, at picking out a trail. And now . . . Sometimes, Grimnir felt his balance slipping in the saddle or as he walked, his lopsided sight skewing the world off-kilter. Much the same, he feared, was happening to his mind.

'Embrace it,' Reginbrand offered. 'Consider it a sacrifice. An eye for an eye, the good book says. An eye to expatiate your sins.'

Grimnir growled low in his throat, and watched the greedy flames eat up the branch. What was it that kept him up, this night of all nights? There was something in the air. Something more than smoke and cinders.

᛬

'There!' Leif pointed, and the three of them pulled on their reins. Not that they could risk more than a slow walk in the curious not-quite-dark. All of them peered beyond Leif's finger, to where a steep shelving of forest blanketed a hillside. One splintered stump of oak stood proud from mossy rocks, scorched and blackened by some long-past lightning strike. Beyond it, shadows crept from a crinkled gully.

'How did you say you found this place again?' said Astrid, narrowing her eyes. She hated the very thought of caves, the press of earth and stone, being trapped.

'I asked the trees,' Leif said.

'Come on,' said Jaska, slipping from her saddle. 'Behind some ferns, you said?' They all dismounted, and led their horses past the blasted oak, deeper and ever deeper into a narrow gorge, thick with bracken, walls of rock and earth rising above them. And then there were ferns, huge ferns, reaching from either side, twice the height of a man – higher, even – and screening an enormous yawn of blackness, the swallowing mouth of what they had sought: a cave.

'Some cave,' whispered Astrid. 'We'll have no problem getting the horses in!' And with a rasp of steel, she drew the Toledo sword. Who knew what might lurk beyond the living curtain?

'I'll sweep our tracks,' said Jaska, dropping back to brush away the traces of their passing. The others pressed on through the ferns, which yielded to the touch, springing back as they went by to mask the travellers and their horses. 'Perfect,' said the little Sami, coming up behind them. The single word, soft as it was, rang from the rock around them.

'Leif – some light?' said Astrid, and he produced the metal clasp he had used before, at the stone circle, whispering it into a soft white gleam that spread around them, washing away the shadows. And three jaws dropped on the instant. Jaska was no stranger to these parts, and Leif and Astrid were Norse through and through, yet none of them had seen anything like it before.

It was like a cathedral.

Back and back stretched the cave, walls arcing out of reach of the light. A vast and vaulted cavern that rose far and away, beyond and above, pillared with twists of solid stone that stood about in spindled columns – others, incomplete, that jutted up and bore down, sharp as rows of monstrous teeth. To one of these they tethered their mounts, the horses already shying, baulking at the enveloping dark. Moving through the cave, they came on fluted ceilings, deep recesses, walls of rock as whorled and sheer as marble. Tapestries of lichen revealed their muted palette to the wan white light. A strange architecture of rock drapes, rock arches, hung high overhead, at once menacing and oddly beautiful. Their feet trod a musty carpet of moss and mushroom, dank and soft.

'It could go on forever,' said Astrid at last, feeling someone had to say something, or they might never break the spell of silence, the cold hush of the place, that settled around them like snow. Her words resounded clear from the cavern walls, the first noise they had heard in what felt like days.

'Nothing goes on forever,' whispered Jaska, and pressed on, Leif at her shoulder. The glimmer of his light played on stranger things, piles of bones and antlers, weird skeletal structures of the dead, rising almost like trees. The stale cave smell thickened in their nostrils. Someone, or something, must have lived – or be living? – here. A something that fed even on elk.

'A bear?' whispered Jaska.

Leif shrugged. 'I hope so,' he said. There was a note of tension in his voice. The wonder of the cavern and the sense of being hidden had driven all thought of the pursuit from their minds, and everyone had begun to relax. But the bone-trees and the rank smell of death spelt a new danger.

Astrid shivered, adjusting her grip on her sword hilt. She had known something like this before – the smell, the mushrooms, the dark and the danger – in Thorbjorn's hut at Hellir. Only the blessed size and sense of space, without which she could hardly breathe, was different. To her mind, a bear would be bad enough.

'Look,' said Jaska, laying a hand on Astrid's shoulder. 'Lights!'

Ahead, two clumps of amber light were hovering, higher than their heads. 'They look like eyes,' Leif muttered.

'What is it about the dark that always brings out the worst of your imagination?' said Astrid. 'They're probably torches.'

But the truth was stranger still. 'Fireflies!' said Jaska, craning her neck. Two glimmering balls of what looked like gold thread, spun into a fine mesh, were suspended from the cavern roof. And in them, their soft light shining through the tiny gaps in the thread, there buzzed about two swarms of fireflies. 'They're beautiful,' Jaska breathed.

'But who,' said Astrid, 'put them there?'

Leif went on. 'The cavern narrows here,' he called back. 'The floor slopes up. And – ow!' He broke off. The others hurried to him.

'An attack?' said Astrid.

'No,' said Leif, rueful. 'I stubbed my toe.' They had come to the end of the cave: a single chamber of rock, almost circular in shape. Moving about, each found something, calling out their discoveries.

'There's a fire laid here,' said Astrid. 'And the rock's blackened right up the wall. There must be hundreds of years' worth of soot here.'

'There are great stones in the centre,' said Jaska. 'This massive long obelisk as high as my head, and this wide, round one beside it . . . The top's almost polished smooth.'

'A great nook has been cut into the wall,' said Leif. 'From roughly level with my shoulders, up. And –' he felt about above him – 'it's lined with furs and pelts. No bear did this. In fact,' he said, 'I think these *are* bear skins. I wonder who's been living in this cave.'

Astrid shrugged. 'I'm too tired to waste good sleeping time in guesswork. It's deserted now, that's the main thing. Let's make the most of it.' And, slender arms straining, she hoisted herself up onto the plinth Leif had found, turned, and hauled Jaska after her. 'There's enough room for all of us to sleep here,' she said. 'It's quite comfortable.' She was in a greater hurry to sleep than she let on. A proper night's rest might bring the dream of flying again. This time, if it lasted, she might be allowed to look upon *his* face. It was what she longed for.

Leif did not attempt to follow her. 'I feel as if somebody should keep watch,' he said. 'I'll go and take the first shift if you like.'

'All right,' called Jaska, from their bunk above. 'Be sure to wake us well before morning!'

Leif made his way back to the cave mouth, settling down with his back against a broad column of rock. The faintest hint of unending twilight fogged the edges of the darkness around him. Leif narrowed his eyes against the half-light. But all he could see was Issar's face. And all he could feel was alone.

CHAPTER THIRTEEN

Leif came awake scarcely knowing he had slept, blinking away the light of an early, early dawn. His tunic was sodden with dew, and the air around felt oddly empty. No birds were singing. *How can it be light already*, a part of his mind thought, and another – the part that had been beaten quiet by loss, by tiredness, by the magic of the wood – answered, *The longest day!* But it wasn't the dawn that had woken him. Something was making a great deal of noise, somewhere not far off. Treetops lower down the slope were shaking as if in a wind, though there was none. And the something was coming nearer.

ʳ

Reginbrand nudged the cold ashes with his foot. The fire was dead. Bleary, still three parts asleep, he glanced up at Grimnir. The grey Dane stood over him, holding something in his right hand. With his left, he clutched the staff of fresh-cut ash that had served as a cooking spit, leaning on it to support himself. Looking at his face, the priest realised that what had woken him had been an inhuman howl of pain.

Grimnir held out his hand towards Reginbrand, palm cupped upwards.

'My eye,' said Grimnir. 'It's my right eye.'

Reginbrand stood, stomach churning. 'Your sins,' he stammered. 'Your sins have found you out.'

'To Hel with my sins,' said Grimnir. One side of his face was an open wound. Reginbrand turned away from the awful sight, to see the slumbering guards begin to stir. One half rose, and Reginbrand blinked in surprise. The shock of Grimnir's eye must have made him delirious, for the man seemed to have a wolf's head where his own should be. The wolf-headed man sat upright and stared the priest full in the face, eyes yellow, unblinking. He bared his teeth in a grin and Reginbrand, on the point of swooning, turned back to Grimnir, bitter bile and a question both rising in his throat.

Grimnir licked his lips, savouring the blood – his own – that had trickled down upon them. The wan grey light of the midsummer dawn fell upon the stick in his left hand. With his one remaining eye, he peered at it. The ash pole was thickening, hardening. At its tip, a bud of iron broke forth, blossoming into a pointed leaf of metal.

'Oh look,' he said, stupidly. 'It's a spear.'

And he thrust it into Reginbrand's trembling belly.

↓

Astrid was flying, legs astride Hestur, air rushing through her full-grown hair. The man on the eight-legged horse was above her, beside her, shadow all about her, and she squinted into the too-near sun to glimpse his face at last.

Odin stared back at her from beneath the brim of his wide traveller's hat. He even looked, she thought, rather like her father.

'The time is upon us,' he said. 'I have chosen my champion, my spearman upon earth. He will ride for me, and I will live through him. See through his eyes. No, wait –' and he cackled an old man's cackle – 'his *eye*. But there is still time, pretty one, for *you* to make *your* choice. To ride with us forever, in judgement on those in battle. To be a Valkyrie. It need not be too late. Only send me a sign. Show me, in blood, what is to be your will.'

She stared at him, breathless, afraid. He levelled his spear at her, dripping with red. And as she came awake, the din of disorder all about her, Odin's words rang again in her head. 'Show me, in blood, what is to be your will.'

ᚠ

Leif sprang to his feet, heart racing. The something was almost upon him; it was rippling the trees right ahead. *The others*, he thought, and then, *The horses*. But he couldn't move. He couldn't not look. And so he saw the giant burst out of the trees, club in hand, an elk slung over its shoulder. And the giant bellowed at Leif as it came on.

'Make way, little manling! Move, or you'll be mincemeat. I've no time for trespassers: *the Wild Hunt is coming!*'

CHAPTER FOURTEEN

Reginbrand had once been a child, a little boy loved by parents, riding wild on his neighbour's cow and splashing with friends in the cool waters of the Elbe, but now he was dying in a Swedish forest and the last thing he saw before his senses left him for good was the spread of black wings blocking out the midsummer sun. 'Michael,' he croaked. 'The angel of death is come for me.' He tried to raise a finger in contrition, but the effort was too great and now there was nothing but a dead body, slumped on the forest floor, soaking soft pine needles in its blood.

Grimnir held out his right arm and the raven settled on his wrist. Dumbly, the grey man squinted at the bird. The bird spoke.

'*Greetings to you, Grimnir. Great Odin has chosen. We all bid you welcome, Wild rider, as Huntsman.*'

'We?' said Grimnir. The raven flapped a wing, and Grimnir looked around at his one-time guards. His left eye, unused to working alone, must have been playing him tricks, for he saw both wolves and men at once, flickering, one world atop another, standing before him.

'*You will lead the Wild Hunt. Wise were you to offer this bloodletting to the Thane-lord: the Allfather. He will watch through your eye, wherever you lead us. But first, seal the bargain, by one more sacrifice.*'

'What must I offer?' said Grimnir, but he knew the answer. The bird shuffled round on his wrist, and bent to the open palm. With one swift dart of its head, it plucked at the eye, tossed it up, opened its beak wide – and what had been Grimnir's right eye disappeared down the raven's gullet.

Grimnir reeled. But he felt new strength course through him, felt the open wound on his face knit together, as the bargain was struck. This had been his fate all his life. The greatest hunter in the North: Odin's loyal servant. It was only the last of many sacrifices he had made.

When Grimnir stood upright again, the bird was long gone. It had taken with it the last remnants of the man he had been, his hope and his reason. The thing that had been Grimnir looked at the men – wolves? – men? – awaiting his word. 'Who am I?' he said.

One of the beasts cocked its head on one side, as if puzzled. '*You are the Hunter,*' it said.

'I am the Hunter,' Grimnir repeated. It was enough.

ᚾ

Someone was shouting. Astrid came awake in a mad tumble, Odin's words echoing in her head – *Show me, in blood, what is to be your will* – and the feeling of flight still with her. It was not surprising, she reasoned, a moment later, that she fell off the ledge. 'But by Thor, it hurts!' she said, picking herself up from the cold stone floor, rubbing the bruised side of her bottom.

'Astrid! We have to go!' Jaska dropped lightly to the ground beside her, lithe as a pine marten, and Astrid glared. But then the bellow came again, savage and deafening in that echoing space, a giant's shout for sure – and they both broke into a run.

Astrid blinked. She tried to swallow, but her throat had run dry on the instant.

Sweat was prickling her palms, yet she had to take charge. 'Horses,' she called to Jaska. 'We have to get out. Go. *Go!*'

Out, out – better in the open than trapped in here, the giant's own home. *Stupid*, she thought, angry at herself for not guessing this would happen – he would move better than them in the dark; he would block the entrance. But a giant would be slow, and if only they could get the horses past him . . . They needed a diversion.

Astrid's mind snapped into place, and she broke into a run. Coming to the great bone-sculptures, she aimed a hefty kick at a skull, sending the whole pile toppling in a crazed avalanche of noise. From the wreckage she scooped up a couple of ribs from what had to be a giant elk, tucking one under each arm, grimacing at the unexpected weight. Then she struggled on towards the blur of light and shadows dancing at the cavern mouth – slowly, maybe too slowly.

She glimpsed Jaska, unmounted, fussing over the horses' harnesses, untangling the leading reins – what the Hel was that girl up to now? Didn't she realise this was all about speed? But there was no time to stop. From ahead of her, there came the roaring.

Astrid burst through the swaying ferns, throwing the ribs in front and rolling out, keeping close to the ground, to one side – at all costs, out of the way and unseen. Gathering up her bones again, she hunkered behind a rock, and took in the scene.

The giant was big. Five men high at least – and grown men at that, not striplings like Leif, who was ducking about around its feet. Her gaze flickered about – from its single snaggled tooth, yellow and vicious in a wide, drooling mouth, to boulder-sized fists, with broken nails like shield rims, one fist clutching a rough-hewn club that was still more tree than weapon. A bristling beard, a belt of skulls – some animal, some human – massive feet, bare and gnarled as a mass of roots and threatening to stamp Leif out of existence with every footfall.

Leif was dancing about between its legs, calling out words that Astrid mostly lost under all the thudding and hollering from the rampaging giant. She caught the odd phrase – 'Patient waiters, web-lords, weave as never before,' and 'Blood-thirsting sky-thrummers, thicken the very air,' – and gaped. And she realised the lumbering giant was slower than even she'd bargained for. Every swing of its club, every stamp of its feet, it made as though neck-deep in water. Leif was talking the midges, the spiders, the insects, into casting a net about the giant, and was confusing it, slowing it down.

But it wasn't enough. With a bellow of fury the giant snatched at empty space with its free hand, rending at the fabric of the air. 'Think you can throttle me, throwing spells and word-tricks? I'll break you like a branch, brash little intruder!' And it swung again. Leif leapt back, but an uncut branch, still growing from the club, caught him a raking blow down his side, and he staggered. The giant grinned, moving in for the kill.

Astrid broke her cover, mouth open in a wordless, savage howl. In her right arm she hefted a rib, holding it like a throwing spear, its wickedly sharp end levelled at the giant. It wheeled round to face her, and she launched the bone weapon with all her might.

Astrid was a superb athlete, hardened by years of training, at play with her brother and on duty with the huscarls of Jelling, strengthened by the summer's hard riding. Her balance, her action, was perfect. But she was also a half-grown girl, and the rib was heavy, and though it struck the giant's chest with a sickening thud, it did not pierce it, and the creature barely flinched as it brushed the bone aside.

Astrid paled. But she hurled the second rib all the same – no good – and drew her sword. Better to go down fighting than to run again.

A blur of movement put her off as the giant came on, breaking into an earth-shuddering run. And then out of the corner of one eye, she could see Jaska bursting from the cave mouth. Something hard and sharp whipped against the backs of her calves and she was down, but scrabbling up again almost at once to meet the onrushing giant –

'Astrid, go *left*! *Now!*' shouted Jaska from somewhere ahead and, bewildered, Astrid hurled her body left. A rushing of air like all the winter gales of the world at once behind her and she dived into a forward roll, coming up hard against the gully wall. Then the earth heaved and she was tossed skywards, and now she was falling, falling, only to land – 'Not *again*!' – exactly as she had when first she woke, and she winced twice as hard as she rose.

But she forgot the pain at once when she saw the giant, fallen full stretch on its face, half in and half out of the cave.

'It's still breathing,' said Jaska from the bushes by her side, and Astrid jumped in shock. 'It'll be up again in a minute. At least the horses got a good night's sleep. Let's ride!'

Leif, already in the saddle, was bringing up Hestur, leading him by a handful of mane, and Astrid saw the taut-stretched rope in the grass – the tripwire Jaska must have strung together from the lead reins.

'Yes,' said Jaska, nodding. 'I've seen it done to stop an elk stampede before. But there's no time to get the rope back. We've got to go.'

Behind, they could hear the first moans as the giant came to its senses. But louder still was the shriek of startled agony from Astrid as she swung herself, unthinking, into Hestur's saddle.

'Are you wounded?' said Jaska, as they all turned to her in alarm.

Astrid blushed, shook her head, explained the two falls and the unfortunate double bruise on her buttock.

Leif half grinned for the first time in many days. 'You know what a good Christian would say?'

'Eh?' said Astrid.

'Turn the other cheek!'

'I don't quite –' Astrid began, but Jaska cut them both off. 'In the name of *all* the gods . . . *Look at the sky!*'

They looked. And, with the crash of a hundred hundred giants toppling, the sky tore open.

ᚦ

The sky tore open, and the world rocked. The horses bolted, and they had to fight hard for some time to bring them under control. Then all was still, and the three of them shaded their eyes against the high rising sun, and stared into the midsummer's morning.

A black dot appeared on the sun's surface, splitting into two dots, growing larger at incredible speed – two birds coming out of the east, flying towards them. And this they scarcely noticed, for the sky itself was burning. White flames licked and lapped right across the heavens, spilling outwards in a crest of fire, and storm clouds of smoke billowed, immense, from the edges. Lightning cracked and splintered in those clouds, a dance of deadly static, a hum of energy and a high snapping rhythm of music that made the hair on the backs of the watchers' necks stand on end. How long they stared, none could tell, but at last the fire burnt itself away, leaving a grey mess of ashen ruin where the sky had been, fading into a morning mist.

The two birds were closer now, and they were ravens. More fliers followed in their train. Jaska, first to find the power of speech, slurred a question. 'A *flock* of ravens? Has there been a battle?'

'Those are no ravens. They are hag-riders,' said Leif, in an awed hush. The hag-riders streamed across the sky: a trail of witches, wolf-mounted.

Astrid shook herself into motion. 'They're coming for us,' she said. 'The Wild Hunt' – and all three of them spurred their horses.

'Uppsala makes more sense than ever,' Jaska panted, as they galloped west and north, away from the airborne host. 'A defensible building; a place of safety. We can shut them out whilst Leif finds the right words. And the Hunt is Odin's alone – the other gods of the temple won't like it, won't let him trample right over their holy places.'

'The Allfather inspires jealousy,' said Leif. 'None would wish to let him rule completely . . . But these riders, the witches in the sky, they can't hurt us – they're just the outliers.'

'They can *see* us, can't they?' snapped Astrid. 'They'll have the Vargar on our scent in no time.' And she remembered the heavy wolves, their promise of revenge. But annoyance as well as fear prompted her words. She wasn't sure she quite agreed with Leif's comments about Odin. A strong king was only natural. Jealousy was petty. Wasn't that obvious? 'We need to get under cover of the forest.'

'Too late,' said Jaska, as they sped down the exposed hillside towards the thickening trees. There was a shrill whooping from high overhead, cries and cackles. Glancing up and around, Astrid saw first one, then a dozen witches swoop low, pointing gnarled talons, screeching in glee as they spotted the fleeing riders. Then, mercifully, the lowering boughs of oak and beech shut out the foul sight, and they thundered, hidden, through the sheltering sentinels of the forest.

'If those witches aren't the real hunters,' gasped Leif, struggling with the pace of the mad gallop, 'who *is* hunting? Is it just the Vargar? We can outpace wolves. And they're far behind.'

And Astrid remembered the earlier part of her last dream. '*I have chosen my champion, my spearman upon earth. He will ride for me, and I will live through him.*' She thought of the grey Dane with the wolf's stare, the one who had thrown the spear at Hedeby . . . had tracked them to Sweden . . . had killed Issar with the same spear. 'I think our enemies have just joined forces,' she said. But she didn't explain how she knew, didn't reveal her dream. And though she said the words, she found it hard to think of Odin – Odin, her father's god, to whom she herself had sacrificed with Knut in the grove at Jelling, just a year ago, and who even now was offering her immortal glory – she found it hard to think of *him* as an enemy.

CHAPTER FIFTEEN

Vornir the giant hauled himself up, a bit at a time, till he was sitting, slumped against the entrance to his cave. His knees ached, his ankles smarted, and most of all his head – oh his head! It hadn't throbbed this hard since the morning after that banquet at Utgardloki's feasting hall, and that had been, what, five hundred years ago? In the good days, when he had been young, and giants had been many.

He squinted up at the sky. Getting on for midafternoon. A fine way to spend a midsummer's morn, passed out on your face, on your own doorstep, without even a night's revels beforehand. Just what had all that been about? Those little gnats; those manlings, running around his feet, messing up his cave, reeking to high heaven with that cloying human smell that still hung in the air. A smell sure to lure Odin's hounds straight here; bring the Wild Hunt right to his home.

The Wild Hunt . . .

And Vornir heard it: a many-throated baying as the hunting pack picked up the scent, all too near. Hide. He had to hide.

Vornir tried to rise, but his limbs would not answer. The fall had been worse than he'd thought – one ankle twisted, one arm dangling. Beads of sweat the size of pears prickled his brow and dampened his ship-sized back. Could he crawl? Was there time?

The baying sound was louder now.

†

Grimnir – the thing that once had been man, and was now only hunter, Odin's hand and Odin's eye – rode a red-eyed horse, whose hoofs threshed empty air. They streamed above the ground, riding head high now, neither hoof nor paw set to the earth. Around him rode the Hunt, seven horsemen, stern and tall, calling each to each and sounding horns. And around him ran the pack, seven huge black wolves, Odin's hounds, baying out their bloodlust. And they were the same seven, so that sometimes the wolves called with the voices of men, and sometimes the riders barked and howled. Only Grimnir was silent, the left eye of the storm.

And the clamour rose still louder as the Hunt burst onto a hillside. Grimnir whipped his heavy grey head round to follow the sound, follow the surge of the Hunt. There was something moving, low and massive, behind a blasted stump, between high rocks. Grimnir felt the tension, the straining of his hunters to be unleashed, to chase down, to kill. Unspeaking, he raised his spear on high; thrust it forward.

116

With a crazed whooping and growling, the seven broke forward, Grimnir in their midst. He saw it plain now, a giant, crippled and crawling, back bared, defenceless. His lip curled. Giants were the other, they were foe – and rightful prey. He saw the giant turn its head, grotesque, one-toothed; saw the fear in its stupid little eyes. And Grimnir's smile spread as the seven leapt, and bore the quarry down with piercing spears and rending teeth.

ᚱ

A bellowing, far behind the three fugitives, borne on the wind, clawed at the day with its anguish. Leif's eyes widened. 'What in Hel's name – ?'

The roaring rose to an unbearable intensity, the pain of ages in their ears, and around it there burst a Hel's din of howls and hollers, like waves crashing on a storm-struck rock. They bore the bellow down until, once more, all was quiet.

Astrid voiced their thoughts. 'The Hunt has found that giant,' she said, her voice small.

'I wish they hadn't,' said Jaska. 'He was only protecting his home, after all.'

'Perhaps he'll take a few of them with him?' said Leif. 'Though the tales don't tell of fallen hunters.'

'What *do* they speak of?' said Astrid. 'There might be something that we've overlooked.'

'Well, for one thing, the Hunt rides in the air,' said Leif.

'*Brilliant*,' sighed Astrid. 'As if it wasn't hard enough already.'

'I don't know,' said Jaska. 'It might help. Harder to follow a scent if you can't put your nose to the ground. Harder to spot a trail, too. We might make use of that.'

Leif, near exhausted as he bobbed about on the cantering horse, was drifting, his mind wandering. 'Just imagine, being able to fly,' he said.

Astrid didn't answer. She had no need to imagine. She had flown in her dreams for many nights now, and one thing she knew: it felt better than this.

ᚱ

'And one last thing: they do not need to sleep.'

In a bid to keep them from dozing in their saddles – and so taking a branch to the face, or falling off altogether – Leif had been recounting every scrap of legend he could dredge up about the Hunt. It was late. Further south, or earlier in the year, night would long since have fallen, but here and now it was still light and the baying of Grimnir's pack rang ever louder from the forest behind them. At this final word from Leif, Jaska broke into a bitter laugh, then cut it short, darting a worried glance at the others. Even to her, it had sounded more than half crazy.

Leif was nearly spent. That day, he had gone from feeling like a player in a game – a deadly game, for sure, but still a race – to feeling like what he knew he was: a hunted animal. The Great Temple no longer shone in his mind as a prize to be won, a place of reckoning, perhaps triumph. Now, it was a den, a shelter, a pitiful place of possible safety. A pitiful place of possible safety. Pitiful possible pittable possaful . . .

He jolted upright, peeling open his eyes. They had all stopped, and a new sound filled his ears: the rushing of water. Leif looked down. He was almost on the edge of a narrow gorge, above a deep, fast-flowing river.

Jaska scratched her head. 'We can't ford it. And we'd go well out of our way going around; we could lose a whole day, and they're catching us all the time. I'd forgotten about this one. Sorry.'

Leif and Astrid exchanged a glance. It was the first time they'd looked properly at each other for a long, long time. And something snapped in both their heads, and they smiled broad smiles.

'No,' said Astrid. 'This is where we start *thinking*.' Odin, she thought, might be god of the Hunt – but he was also a god of tricks and scheming. It was time to pay him in kind.

'Since we've stopped, we may as well get some food,' said Leif. 'All six of us are starving as it is.'

'We've no time to *catch* anything!' said Jaska. 'And as for foraging . . .' She swept her hands around the glade of trees at the river's edge. All were oaks: an ancient stand of mighty trees, their roots cradling the brink of the gorge.

But Leif wasn't listening. He had slipped from his horse, and wandered over to the oldest, hoariest oak in sight, its bark silvered with age and scored deep from boar tusks and bear claws. Tenderly, respectfully, Leif laid a hand on its trunk. 'The shelterer of Thor, thunder-guard, rememberer, would not wish that such as we should starve among plenty.'

And then he bent closer to a whorled hole in the trunk, and whispered still more secret things.

A pause. A silence. And then, with a slow and stately rustle, all the trees around them bent their heads, branches bowing to the travellers. At their tips were small, round burdens.

'Acorns?' said Astrid.

'Oak apples!' laughed Jaska, jumping up to seize one. And before their eyes, a hundred acorns swelled and ripened, casting off their crinkled cups, and a harvest of apples began to fall, lightly, to the ground.

'Thank you,' whispered Leif, moving to the edge of the cliff. His stomach was rumbling in anticipation, but he couldn't give in yet. There was more to be done. He shouted down at the waters. 'Taper-tailed net leapers! Thor's catch; trickster's refuge! Come to me, shape-shifters – sacrifice is noble.' And even Astrid, well used to Leif's marvels, goggled in wonder, as three fat salmon burst forth from the river, to fall, slick and still, at their feet.

As lighting a fire was unthinkable, the ravenous fugitives seized the fish in their hands, slitting the skin free with pocket knives and tearing into the bright, cool flesh, more flame-coloured than pink, and alive with the taste of freedom. The horses chomped down on their feast of apples. And for once, the sunlight that still shone through the oak leaves bathed them all in a rich, warm glow, and their hearts – and stomachs – were at peace.

'We still have to cross the river,' said Jaska, a little later. 'And even if we could swim it, those hag-riders roaming around the sky would spot us for sure.'

They were full, rested, almost happy – the odd howl showed that the Hunt was closing in, but what was the prospect of an imminent and violent death, next to the enjoyment of a good meal, long overdue?

'Don't worry,' said Astrid, stifling a yawn. 'We've thought of that.' And she pointed, fingers still smeared with fish and apple juice, to Leif, then back to herself.

'But you haven't said a word,' began Jaska, and then stopped. She was just grateful that they seemed to be something like friends again. Who knew if it would last? But best not to push at it.

Astrid had her harp already on her lap, tricking out a slow, dancing melody, the bass never changing, so the music hung in the air, building, building, never quite advancing, on the edge of something happening. *Thrum*, went the low notes. *Thrum thrum thrum*. And with a free finger, Astrid tapped out a soft rumbling rhythm on its wooden body.

Jaska, swaying slightly to the music, suddenly blinked in confusion. A drop of water had landed on her arm. Spray from the river? She looked up.

The midsummer sky was thick with clouds. In another instant, they would throng across the face of the sun.

'Sing!' cried Astrid. 'Sing me a wind, to blow those witchy watchers away!'

Leif cocked an eyebrow. When she was caught up in the weather-magic, he thought, she started talking a lot more like he did.

But Jaska stood, turned her face to the sky, and sang. There were no words to her song. Her face was open and shining, cheeks red, and the sound was strangely low and guttural for one so small: breathy and billowing. Soon her hair was whipping in a strong wind, and the clouds were racing across the hidden sun; all was dark and gusting. Leif, eyes wide against the sudden gloom, could just make out the tumbling of tiny figures blown westwards on the gale, and above the noise of wind and song, the thinnest, crossest shrieks from those far-flung watchers.

Astrid laid down her harp, stood, saw – and danced for joy, jigging on the spot.

'Such *power*,' she said, and she sounded far away as she said it. 'To command the elements . . .'

'We've still got to ford the river,' Jaska pointed out, returning to herself, still a little flushed and giddy. She felt like swallows were swooping inside her, but her wood-wise instincts were strong. 'They'll have heard our music. We have to move!'

'The opposite: we have to have *stillness*,' said Leif, his voice quiet against the high roaring of wind and water. He turned back to the river, away from the others, a frown knitting his brows together. He had to think himself out of summer, out of this mad rush. He thought back to the last winter, to the snow on King Gorm's grave, to the heavy-laden skies. The stillness of forests, and skaters on Lake Faarup.

But despite his efforts, and despite the cool, fresh meal that soothed at the gnawing edges of his hunger, Leif could not turn the memories to words. Things got in the way: Issar's death, the sticky heat of fear-scented sweat, the constant itch of a hundred marks on his gnat-bitten ankles, the far-off look in Astrid's eyes, unreachable, maddening . . . Issar's death, saddle sores, the savage boiling rush of a summer where blood and howls rose on the haze, Issar's death – and Leif opened his mouth to speak to the river, and all that came out was,

'Let it *stop*!'

A single tear of pure frustration rolled up and out of the corner of his eye, welled onto the tip of a straight, dark lash, and fell from his face to meet the river below.

Where instantly, it froze.

Leif blinked. He had *done it*. Somehow, he had done it – had failed, failed entirely, to capture the truth of the river, but had shared with it *his* truth. He yearned for calm, for quiet, for a healing over and a return to other times. And the river, understanding, had responded. Below them, stretching away down the gorge on either side, was a wide and gleaming band of ice.

'That was well done,' said Astrid, coming up. 'Is it safe?' And, not waiting for an answer, she leapt down onto the icy surface, sliding half across its width in a low crouch, two streaks of dust left by her long leather boots.

Grinning, Astrid turned back, to see two expectant faces looking down at her.

'Not a crack!' she said. 'It's solid right through. If we fasten some sacking round the horses' hoofs, we can be off in no time.' And she hauled herself back up over the cliff. It was good to be in charge, good to be taking action, not just mindlessly fleeing. This was *strategy*. Who knew – *he* might even approve. And besides, she had always loved ice skating.

Soon they were all on the strange, glassy river, skittering and slipping like newborn foals – the horses especially. In the unnatural darkness, the summoned wind still whipping through their hair, the ghostly glow of the ice and the summer forest all around made for a dizzying mix, and no one quite knew whether to laugh or flinch at every step.

'So: straight across then?' said Astrid.

'No,' said Jaska, and now she did smile. 'This is our chance to throw them off. No tracks, no scent – they'll be stumped when they get to the bank! It'll be as if we just sprouted wings and took flight. And if we've seen the last of those sky-riders, we can reach Uppsala before they work out where we've gone.' And she took the lead downriver – downhill, as it now was – leading her wide-eyed, snorting horse in a giddy, sliding shuffle.

Leif, following, tried to think ahead. 'The Hunt never lasts more than one full moon,' he said. 'We can simply shelter in the temple, and wait it out until the Hunt's called off.' It was a good plan, he knew. So why did he sound dissatisfied even to himself as he said it? He wasn't so vain as to long for a final reckoning, a display of his skill in a place of power – better by far, he knew, not to risk things. Revenge? Revenge for Issar? Was that what he wanted?

Astrid said nothing. She too had been relishing the thought of a last stand, a chance to turn and fight, to prove herself no coward. Was it honourable to take refuge, to avoid battle? Surely not. And even if it worked, what then? If Birka and the Swedish court was still in league with Haralt, still out for their blood, then where were they to turn? Surely she couldn't be expected to spend her life in the forest – no glory, no fame . . . come to that, no combs and no jewellery, which she'd never thought she'd miss before – but maybe that was what Leif wanted? To write poems to the trees and live in moss-roofed huts. Surely death was preferable to such a shameful existence. But she couldn't say any of this out loud. The others, love them though she did, didn't really understand about things like honour.

'This'll do,' said Jaska, breaking across both Leif's and Astrid's thoughts. 'We don't want to go too far out of our way.' They had come to a shallow stretch of the north bank, all rock, root and shingle up to the treeline. Jaska waved the others off the river, and they guided the horses gingerly onto proper ground. Jaska led her own mount into the trees, then carefully swept the trail, replacing every overturned stone. 'Leif?' she said.

He whispered to the frozen water – 'And set it free' – hoping it would release the tangled knot that sat inside him. And he watched the ice begin to break, the trickle of meltwater, the crack and flow, the swell and the torrent – and knew the ice within him to be as firm and hard as ever.

A howl of fury rose from somewhere on the far bank, upstream. 'Time to go,' whispered Astrid, urging Leif and Jaska silently to their horses. She lingered a moment longer in the shadow of the forest, then went to Hestur. There would be hard riding ahead of them.

'Have we thrown them off?' said Jaska, as they rode. 'Can they cross the river if they ride above the ground?'

'I don't know,' said Leif. 'I think they have to ride over the earth, even if they never truly touch it – running water is a powerful force, and tends to break the effects of magic. But this is Odin's Hunt . . . I just don't know.'

'Well at least, if nothing else,' said Jaska, 'we should have won enough time for some sleep.'

Until recently, none could have imagined sleeping with a sound as terrible as the baying pack in their ears, even from a long way off. But then, until recently, none of them had really known what it was to be tired.

CHAPTER SIXTEEN

'Don't think I'm not impressed,' said Odin.

They were snatching a short sleep, the horses resting while still saddled, and taking turns to listen for signs of pursuit. Right now Jaska was sitting up, pale and shivering, and looking very small, listening to the ragged-edged howls and horn-calls from the south. Some near, some further off, moving, circling – the Hunt must have spread out along the river, searching for the point where the quarry could have crossed it. But now the cries were gathering, rising in pitch – Jaska could scarcely believe it – as if a wolf had found their trail. But how? They had been so careful. Should she wake the others? Or were her addled senses playing tricks?

Astrid, lost in sleep, was again riding the sky. Beside her, larger than ever, power and impatience crackling off him like sparks from a raging fire, rode the Allfather.

'Don't think I'm not impressed,' he said. 'And don't think I don't know. I may not be able to see you, little runners, but these are my lands, and I can feel the working of strong magics. To shut out the light of my own kin, Sol – to sweep the riders from the sky, oak to apple and summer to winter – you roll your dice well, girl, you and that accursed silver-tongued upstart.' He broke off, as his eight-legged steed tossed its head, frothed and foamed, rearing. It was as if he was struggling to rein in his own anger. 'You have turned nature on its head,' he went on. 'Toppled the natural order! It shows the spirit I look for in a shield maiden.' And Astrid swelled with pride.

'But I am the lord of order,' Odin said. 'It is mine to command: my duty, and my reward. And if you wish it upset – if that is the game we are to play – then so be it.' He grinned, the same deranged wolf's grin her father Gorm had cracked when he announced that he had gone blind, only a year ago.

'Then so be it,' Odin cackled. 'Let there be . . . *chaos*!'

The serene sky of the dream plummeted away, and Astrid felt herself wheeling, free-falling, through a cloud of storms. Lightning rent her world, and he was gone – there was only the forest floor, and driving rain, and the panicked faces of the others, all awake in the same moment, and all cowering under the roll of a thunder that rocked the sky like an erupting volcano; a thunder that shook a world turned to nightmare.

⸸

Grimnir threw back his head and howled at the moon, joining the exultant chorus of the Hunt. For a moon it was that hung in the sky, no longer a midsummer sun, a moon wreathed with thick black clouds, and the thunder and lightning thrilled through their lean, taut bodies.

He flung the spear across the river, and in its path there fell a tree, broad as a bridge. The hunters swarmed across it, sped into the forest and away, and Grimnir rode after them, the tree vanishing behind the red-eyed horse's hoofs. He plucked the spear, still quivering, from the tree where it had struck – a young tree, an alder, with one low branch snapped off, telltale, as if from the passing of a cantering horse. It had been the sign, the trace of the prey, that he had needed – just when all signs seemed to have gone. And now his wolves were hunting in the pitch of night, and death was on the wind. The Hunt was good. Let there be thunder! Let there be lightning! Let there be chaos!

†

'They've found us,' said Jaska. *'Ride!'*

The horses needed no prompting. As soon as the familiar weights were on their backs, they bolted, running north. The thunder had spooked them, but there was something more – the Hunt was on the wind – and the forest was not what it had been before they slept.

'This is a terrible ride.' Leif spoke for them all. It was not just dark, it was night, and a hunter's moon hung high above the raging storm. As the riders streaked by on panicked horses, nostrils flaring, the branches of once-friendly trees turned to traitors, reaching out, plucking at them with skeletal fingers, snagging and raking, drawing blood. Roots snaked up, twisting, sinuous, to trip and clutch at horses' shanks. And every tall tree caught in the moon gleam was the shadow of a gibbet.

Leif tried not to look, tried not to see – the shapes and shadows were crazed and crooked, capering at the edge of his sight and his mind – but to close his eyes would mean to career right into the next trunk looming up ahead, misshapen ghosts and goblins . . .

They were no longer a group, three friends together: each was lost and alone in their terror. An owl took flight from a hawthorn tree and Leif saw the heavy wings of the Beast, the shining, screaming angel that had risen on the moon, that had shattered the Yelling Stones and had stalked his every dream. The flash of eyes in shrouded bushes were those of Garm, the *Hel*-hound, who had lurked beside the river . . .

Jaska was a babe again, abandoned in a foreign town. The cruel trees were crushing strangers, the shadows those of city walls. The creep and brush of branches down her back were Ginnarr's nails or those of his men, whilst beyond, the savage gods of her homeland stalked the storm. Stallo, the devourer, hulking and horrid. Ruohtta, the death-rider, and pestilence would spread in the wake of his horse. Leibolmai, the hunter, on whose whim the fate of every hunted animal was decided and who surely ran with their pursuers. A hunter worshipped by tall, hard-faced men, like the one who used to beat her mother and kicked the children from his path . . .

Astrid was not afraid. The words went round and round her head. Not afraid. Not afraid. She alone knew what was happening, and that had to count for something, surely? Odin had taken her into his counsel – so none of this was really meant for her. Excitement alone must be racing through her limbs, setting them trembling – and exhaustion, of course, which was why her mind preyed on that moment, a winter away now: the moment in the Great Hall, the moment she had heard the news of her darling brother's death. The moment her world had fallen away and her heart had stopped.

She wrenched her head free of the thought. *Concentrate*, she told herself. *Pass the ordeal. Play the game.* Valkyries had to be brave, didn't they? Had to be free from the dread of mortals, if they were to watch on, serene, at battle after battle. And to remind herself what fear *really* looked like, she was about to turn and look at Jaska, riding at her side. Was about to turn – when another thought, unbidden, struck her.

What if the rider in the dark, in the night – what if the rider at her side, wasn't Jaska after all?

What if the person on that horse had changed without her seeing? What if they were no longer a person?

For a long, long time, Astrid stared fixedly ahead. On the edge of her vision, faint in the moonlight, the head and shoulder of another horse. The pounding noise of its gallop. And on its back, within touching distance of her – who knew?

For shame, Astrid, she thought. And turned.

An empty skull leered back at her – a pointed skull, its hanging jaw enormously long, a dog-headed skeleton reaching out a bony claw –

'Astrid? *Astrid*, are you all right?!'

131

Astrid blinked, and Jaska, ashen-faced, was a handspan away, clutching her swooning body. Their horses had stopped. She had almost fallen from the saddle.

'This is a terrible ride,' Leif said again.

|

None of them knew how much of it was real. But they all heard the revelry of witches, dimly dancing in the distance, and saw the glow of their green fires. All felt the loom overhead, above the canopy, of the giant cloud eagle, storm-bringer, corpse-swallower, black and shadow-formed, iron-beaked with swords for talons. Heard its piercing cry and felt the buffets of its mighty wings; had it prey long on their minds. And the storm-tossed, night-racked riders all saw it when a hare shot into their path, closely followed by a great red stag, crowned with lordly antlers, and running at full pelt.

'It seems that it is not just us who flee,' said Leif, as the three horses came up short in shock. But he was as silent as the others as he saw the stag open a mouth of needle-sharp teeth, and stretch down its neck to snatch the hare in its jaws, shake it as a dog shakes a rat, tear at its flesh. As they stared, aghast, the stag turned to face them, flanks heaving, mad-eyed. It pawed the ground, flared its nostrils . . . and charged, head lowered, straight at them . . . only to vanish at the moment it should have struck.

'And now all nature is turned upside down,' said Leif, his voice trembling on the edge of reason.

'Did we do this,' said Jaska, 'with our meddling?'

'The last thing that we need right now is to start feeling guilty,' said Astrid.

They rode on. What else was there to do?

†

Once, there had been a man called Kenulf Sigmundsson. He had sat on Haralt's benches, eaten his bread, worn his gold, and held firm when brother had faced brother in that hot, horrible summer of the angel and the priest. Kenulf was one of Haralt's most trusted huscarls, savage and loyal, and one of the first the new king had turned to when seeking an escort for Grimnir's mission. And when they had sailed from Hedeby, Kenulf had left behind him a fat little wife and three strong children, two of them old enough to know him and to well with tears as they waved goodbye.

But none of that mattered now, for the Hunt had claimed him and the wolf inside had risen.

And tonight his blood was up. He had tasted giant, tasted elk, and now he was wolf-hungry for the taste of human flesh. The quarry's scent was on the wind, fear and sweat, man and horse, pale limbs, hot innards.

His world was one of smell and shadow. In the pallid light of the hunter's moon, everything ran grey and brown, dull shapes of tree and heath. His prickled ears were full of thunder, the noise of the chase and the noise of the sky, crackling lightning and the clamour of his brothers. But the *smells* were raw red threads of scent pulling him on, ever on, and his paws slapped the empty air above the trail, and his snout thrust forward, and –

And Kenulf was in charge again, a horse-borne rider, a horn to his lips and a spear slung across his back. They were huntsmen, they had names, clothes, histories, and the Hunt was a world of colour and sound, not scent. Still, his own name lay beyond his reach, his own past before the Hunt a mystery – had he not always lived like this, riding to hounds, riding through forests, chasing an eternal prey? Prey and pines and pounding blood, coldness of night, heat of the chase, running with the gait that ate up the ground, never tiring, always hungry, the pack about him, the prey before him . . . And he raised his muzzle, opened his jaws, and howled his hunger at the moon.

This wolf was strong, it was eager, keen, yearning, and it broke free of the pack with a renewed surge of urgency. They were close now. So close. Let it be the first! It turned a plaintive head back to Grimnir, the master, and whined a question.

The grey spearman stared at the wolf. Weighed up its gaunt belly, ragged flanks, matted pelt; but also its barrel chest, heavy paws, powerful shoulders; and above all, its ravening yellow eyes. It might well do.

Grimnir nodded once, and the wolf whipped about and sped forward like an arrow unleashed, tearing ahead of the pack and out of sight – the first barb the Hunter had hurled at the chase. Let it find its mark!

CHAPTER SEVENTEEN

How did the Hunt keep finding them? How did they know where to cross the river? You can't follow a scent across water, and Jaska had swept the path clear so carefully – for that matter, they had swept the *sky* clear! Leif and Jaska threw the question back and forth as they rode, knowing it was pointless, but knowing that talking was the only way to stay sane, to stay awake – to stay alive.

'However they managed it, they're on our scent now,' Jaska said at last. 'Which means we can't stop, can't sleep, and we're slowing down. It's not far now – that was the last river to cross. I'm just afraid that, without time for one more stop to regain our strength, we'll be overrun, even if it's within sight of the temple – caught on the burial mounds themselves! And we need to keep our lead if we want to fortify the place, bar the doors.'

She was rambling, she knew it, and her words were whipped about by the gale, but it didn't stop them being true. She was about to press her point home, when Astrid reined in Hestur and held up her hand. But surely, this was no place to stop. The trees thronged thick, with enough undergrowth to hide an attacker, and they stood at the wrong end of a low rise, downhill from their pursuit. Reluctantly, the others drew up, horses bucking, uneasy, straining to be off, to keep running. They knew all too well what was behind them.

'What is it?' said Jaska, bracing herself for some fresh horror ahead.

'I'm not . . . it's just . . .' said Astrid, distractedly. She was busy wheeling Hestur around, urging him to turn back. 'I thought I heard something – sensed something.' And she reached for her sword-hilt.

'But you can hear the Hunt,' Leif protested. 'They're still some way off.' The baying of ravenous throats was louder than ever, but he was right: it was still behind them. This was madness. 'I'm going on,' he said, and touched his heels to his horse's sides, so that it began to push past Astrid, knocking her off balance in the act of drawing her blade – and so that their backs were turned to the night behind them.

And from the night it came. Jaska saw it, and to her addled mind it was as if the spectral shape of a rider was toppling out of the dark towards them, spear raised. But then it was a wolf, a wolf that poured from the darkness like oil from a pitcher, a wolf near as big as a horse, red throat, teeth knocking. It sprang straight at Leif, Jaska saw it plain, but the two horses were rearing, Astrid falling across Leif's back. A dun-coloured cloak of rough-sewn cloth covered her shoulders, and above, the thatch of gold, now grown down to her ears. But below her hair was a little wisp, one soft

136

curl like the first growth on a baby's forehead, that played about her bare neck and sometimes tickled her half-crazy, though she never thought to cut it.

And that slim white sliver of neck was where the wolf sunk its fangs.

Astrid screamed, a white-hot pitch of pure pain, as the wolf bit down. She could smell its fetid breath and its great stinking body as it scrabbled over Hestur's hindquarters. The Toledo sword flew from her hand, wheeling to fall, point first, beside Leif. There was slobber and blood oozing down her neck and now she was on the ground and the wolf was above her, heavy pants and guttural snarls. The fall had wrenched its jaws free of her neck and for an instant she could glance about at the dark of the forest floor.

Jaska was nowhere to be seen. Had the girl run? She'd spent years as a thrall, after all, and her people were only herdsmen; you could hardly blame her. But she could see Leif's legs, upside-down, and his hand reaching for her sword.

'Strike, Leif!' she screamed, as the wolf came again, teeth scraping raw at the back of her head, exposing its neck to Leif's blow.

Leif froze. The wolf had hurt his dearest friend, was trying to kill her, and when he snatched up the sword and its jaws closed on her neck, he was ready and willing to drive the blade home. Astrid had taught him what to do. Don't slash with the open edge. It looks good, but it's slow, and weak, the force spreads out along the sword, and you can't control where you hit. Lead with the tip, thrust forward, it's faster, and accurate, and you put all your effort into one place. Below the shoulder, drive through to the heart. And he would do it!

But, 'Strike, Leif!' screamed Astrid, and the animal bent away from him. In that moment it was defenceless, a dumb beast, helpless against his steel. And there danced before his memory that other moment, many moons before, when Folkmar had been pinned, prone before him, and he had held the knife that could have sealed the fate of the North. '*Flesh and blood*,' the Yelling Stones had whispered to him. '*Flesh . . . blood . . .*' And Leif tightened his grip on the sword-hilt, shifted his weight, focused on the spot he would hit – and he hesitated.

'Now, Leif, now!' Astrid screamed, her mouth half choked with mud and leaves.

He had thought himself compassionate, merciful; weary of the endless violence that ended so many lives, but that narrowed still more, blinding men to all that was good and gentle and beautiful. But perhaps, thought Leif, for the first time, perhaps that wasn't what it was. Perhaps he was simply a coward. And he faltered, and the wolf stretched wide its jaws for a final snap that might sever Astrid's spine.

And with a gut-thumping whirr and shunk, the sharp point buried itself in the wolf's heart and it fell down dead.

Leif looked round to see Jaska already notching a second arrow to her bowstring, ready for the beast to rise again. But it didn't. It was over.

'Astrid!' cried Jaska, and went to her, thrusting the huge hairy body off from Astrid's back. Astrid struggled to her feet. Grimaced. 'Help me get a cloth tied tight round this or I'll soon be as white as you. I don't think it bit me too deeply. It's as if it held back. And it wasn't the only one . . .'

She was all right. She really was – hurt, but whole – and there was still some good in the world. They all felt it strike them with the force of a sunbeam. Except Astrid. She mostly felt the screaming holes where the wolf's teeth had punctured her skin.

Jaska went to Leif. Took the sword from his numb fingers, handed it back to Astrid without comment. 'Leif,' she said, and her voice was low, flat, serious. 'We've lost some of our lead, and blood's been spilt. We have to give them the slip; we can't outrun them. I can cover our tracks, but it's no good unless you can cover the scent. Is there anything, any charm, any rhyme, that could help us?'

Astrid's opinion of the Sami girl rose still further. She could kill a wolf, and she could think fast enough to turn Leif's attention from his cowardice, put him to use, save his face. After some thinking and muttering whilst Jaska swept the trail, Leif brought forth a poem that filled the air around them with thick, cloying forest smells – sap, roses, apples, honey, lily, currants, berries, hawthorn, pine, honeysuckle – a smell that rose and spread and had them retching and dizzy from the strength of it. Astrid nodded at Jaska, forgetting how much the tilt of her neck would hurt her. The spell would work. And it had helped Leif regain some pride. But she still couldn't bear to look at him. 'You two take the lead,' she said. 'I'm fine – really, I'm fine. And I'd best bring up the rear in case of any more overeager hunters.'

Astrid lingered for a few moments before following the others at a brisk trot. But not long enough to see the dead wolf's fur melt away, and its lengthy muzzle recede, to leave, lying dead on the trampled, matted floor of a sweet-reeking, benighted Swedish forest, the lonely figure of Kenulf Sigmundsson.

ᚻ

A little later, Grimnir looked down on Kenulf's corpse, the arrow rising straight from his back. 'I missed my mark,' the Hunter said, and his voice was Odin's ancient, unkind rasp. 'I missed my mark, and broke my spear. The next throw will be better, for it will have all my force behind it.' He paused. 'But the Hunt should profit by its mistakes.' He raised his voice. 'Eat,' he said.

Whilst the six remaining wolves ravened on the flesh of their former brother, Grimnir sniffed the air. Wrinkled his nose. Some new ruse: the prey had masked its scent. He stared about, using all of his former self's skill to search for telltale signs. But the path had been swept clean. It stopped here.

His eye narrowed. For some time he was lost in contemplation as his hunters feasted. It had never failed. Not once in a hundred years had the Hunt lost its quarry. And *he* – he was Odin's vessel! It was unthinkable that the Allfather, the Ancient, the Wise, the High One, should be bested by a dark-skinned little skald and a Lapp slave, even if they did have the help of a powerful and royal-born shield maiden. *Unthinkable*.

Enraged, he drove his balled fist against a tree trunk, with such force that he buried his hand in the wood.

When he withdrew the hand, he was frowning. A little below the hole he had made, there were runes etched into the bark. Crudely carved, as if in haste. Not the elegant long-branch runes that were chiselled into standing stones, but the quick, scrappy, short-twig runes used for leaving messages in wood. Grimnir stared at them.

ᚢᚦᛁᛋᛅ

'Uppsala', read the runes. And Grimnir smiled.

CHAPTER EIGHTEEN

Haralt Bluetooth was reading too. A year ago he could read only runes, and at first his struggles with the brittle pages and the looping Latin script had been as hard as any with his brother Knut, or on the battlefield. But he knew these books were important. You could put the whole world in a book. And not just the world as it existed, but the world as you wanted it to be.

Now he had in his hands Bishop Leofdag's pages: the tales he wished to tell about the northern pagans. The atrocities it contained were shocking, but more than that: they were absurd. No Dane would believe a word of it. But a German, an Italian, or a Frank would.

It amazed Haralt, this power that lay in words. Told right, a lie could be more real than the truth. He thought of the runes he had etched into the Yelling Stones. Their boast that he had united Denmark as a Christian kingdom. It had been a lie. But by writing it into the stones, he had made it real.

And as he read the lies Bishop Leofdag had written about

the Great Temple at Uppsala, and what people did there, Haralt thought: *They are not lies once they're written down. People will read them, and people will believe them. And then they'll be more real than the truth.* With a well-told tale, you could change the world forever.

↑

Nearly there. Nearly there, and Jaska felt its pull. If she could get them there, and get them there first – perhaps, even, without being followed – then she would truly have proven herself to these dazzling new friends. The brilliant, witty, impossible boy, and the girl that shone like a second sun. The closest she had known to a family in many years. Get out of this, and she could return to her people with her head held high – the girl who bested the Wild Hunt! The Sami who outwitted the cruel god of the Norsemen. Get out of this, and she would have a choice, for the first time in her life. Maybe she would stay with these new friends; seek new adventures. But first came the hard part: *getting out of this.*

Leif was tingling all over, brimming with he hardly knew what feelings. Only let them reach the temple first, let them turn and face the Hunt with the strength of the ages behind Leif's words, and he would show them he was no coward. The blade was not his weapon – and so? It made him no less of a warrior. He whetted his lips. Time to talk these bloody-minded brutes into defeat. The skald's victory! And in defying Odin, and winning, might he not also win back Astrid? She had gone so far away from him in this horrible Hunt.

Astrid's teeth nibbled and tore, worrying the edge of her lower lip. She still rode last of the party, and her bloodied neck was always twisting, looking behind, looking in front. Only Hestur, hot and weary beneath her, was real, was known, was dependable. Her head was full of death-or-glory final stands, heroes of old, backs to the wall but with undying honour before them. Undying. Her heart, she thought, her *thump-thump-thumping* heart, was too big for her body. It would burst her bones.

Behind them, Grimnir rode amidst the pack, a rattling ribcage of hate and intention. The Hunt was near its end, and his purpose with it. But he did not think of this. In his hand he gripped the spear. The spear was all he knew.

Six loping wolves snarled, whined, bickered. No longer did their forms flit; there were no more riders. The men inside were gone. The wolf had eaten each of them away from within. Six more Danes lost deep in the forest. Victims of the Hunt.

ᚦ

'What happened to the forest?'

All at once they had broken through the treeline. One instant, a shaded throng of trunks, branches, needles all around. The next, their horses' hoofs slammed down onto a moon-glimmered heath. The odd shrub, a lone and twisted tree or two, but, mostly, a bare plain, stark and rolling.

Blasted scrubland, dim in the night's light, stretched before them and, instinctively, their mounts eased their legs into a joyful canter. To be free of the trees!

In the distance, three mounds rose high out of the heath, ghostly humps of darker darkness.

'Uppsala!' cried Jaska. 'The ancient graves!'

Astrid wrinkled her nose. 'Father's is bigger,' she said.

'There's a low valley on the other side,' said Jaska, unheeding. 'That's where the temple lies. I told you we'd get there! I told you!' She was beaming, her blood thrilling to the speed of her horse, the rushing wind, the open sky and the nearness of success.

'And not a sign –' she began.

But her words were drowned in a furious chorus of howling from the forest. Turning, aghast, they saw at first a charcoal smudge: the shadowy mass of trees, too many and too close together to be more than a single blackness.

And then they saw movement, and pinpricks of yellow, as first one, then six wolves burst forth. And behind them, the two red, burning eyes of Grimnir's horse. There was yet one more. The baleful, unblinking dot of Grimnir's lone left eye. Each felt it bore into them. And even from that distance, it felt cold. Hard. And utterly free from pity.

'Ride! Ride for your lives!' Jaska managed, distraught and appalled in her moment of triumph. Still, they had a lead, slim as it was. And no wolf could outrun a horse, if that horse was at full strength.

'Leif,' said Astrid, her mind working to the same rhythm, 'can you give us anything? The horses, I mean?'

Leif blinked.

'Wave-lords of the land-sea!
Leaping, surging coursers!
Best your ocean brothers
By running the stronger!'

Where the words came from, he'd no idea – something about the breakers on waves being 'white horses', something in the tirelessness of the sea – but they had an immediate effect. He tightened his grip as the horses streaked forward with renewed vigour, and the pack fell behind.

'I've got more!' he said, and spoke again, throwing the lines over his shoulder as if they were stones. The bone-dry heath behind them burst at once into a wall of flame, scorching their backs.

'That should hold them!' cried Jaska, but once again, she had spoken too soon. One by one, the wolves leapt high, each clearing the fire. And before her scarce-believing gaze, Grimnir himself crashed his black charger right through the flickering red, and the tongues of flame shrank back from his horse and died to nothing. The Hunt came on.

'Not far to the mounds now,' Astrid panted. They had covered more than half the distance in a staggeringly short time, but madder still, the Hunt was gaining on them, spurred into a fury by Leif's attempts at resistance; the fury of a god not used to being answered back.

'We need more time, or they'll catch us at the very door,' said Jaska. Risking another glance back, she could see

Grimnir half rising from his saddle, flexing his spear-arm – the arm that had slain Issar. Not close enough to chance a throw. But not far off either.

'Never fear. Just get us to the mounds first,' Leif called back to her. He felt it now, felt what it was that had lent the strength to his words. The power of Uppsala, the prayers and sacrifices of a kingdom, of the centuries, seeping out and into his poems. Everything was heightened in this place. It set his flesh shivering with potential. He was ready to try anything.

Anything, as long as he could focus on the task in hand, and not look back at the grim grey hunter. But despite himself he glanced over his shoulder and saw that high dead face, ever closer.

He saw something else too. The Hunt had come to ground. No longer were they ripping through the sky, riding the air – wolf paws were slapping the dry, blasted heath, gouging earth with their claws, the red-eyed horse's hoofs tearing up the grass.

Of course – they were out of the forest. This wasn't Odin's domain, not this near the temple. He didn't reign here. It must make them weaker, even as he, Leif, drew strength from the age-old power of Uppsala. The thought gave him hope.

And then he saw a third thing. The Hunt was almost at their heels, and two wolves broke ahead, putting on a spurt, leaping at Hestur. They were worrying at his flanks, screwing themselves clear of his kicking hind legs, dragging him down. Astrid was twisted round in the saddle, hacking at one with her sword, but the angle was impossible.

Leif let out a cry – some unknown couplet, the words flung from his mouth, forgotten on the instant – and the heath split beneath the wolves, a deep chasm opening. One fell instantly from sight, lost to the depths of the earth, a howl of terror left hanging in the cold night air. The other had checked, gathering for a second spring, and found its forepaws scrabbling at the abyss. With a desperate effort it flexed, coiled, wrenched its way back to safety – and Hestur kicked clear, scratched and scared, pelting after the others. The rest of the oncoming Hunt knocked the back-pedalling wolf aside, clearing the gap in a single bound, and it closed up again behind them. But it had gained them some distance. And now Grimnir had only five wolves in his pack.

Enormous black shapes were rearing up on either side, swallowing the sky, and Leif's heart lodged halfway up his throat before he realised that they were speeding between the burial mounds. On the other side was Uppsala. But the Hunt was too close. Could he dredge up one last effort?

And he felt it hit him, the ages of Uppsala, the richness and the sorrow of all that had gone before, all that was and would be – all that had been, and might be again. And he thought of his enemy, Odin, and how long ago he and his brothers had made the world from the butchered body of the first god, Ymir. Ymir's remains were all around them. And the world, Leif thought, was many things. But most of all, it was old.

He tugged hard on the reins, leant back, and the bit dug into his horse's mouth, bringing it up short in spite of its fear. The other two rushed past him, shadowed shapes, riding Hel for leather. But Leif wheeled his horse round, side on, silhouetted against the moon, between the mounds. And with arms held high he stared Grimnir full in his hateful grey face, and shouted at the hills to either side.

'Shoulders of old Ymir,
Overthrow your shackles!
Arise again! Make me
A wall against Odin.'

Then Leif, spent from his exertions, could hold his horse no longer. It shot round and fled the rushing wolves, and he clung tight to keep his seat. In his ears was a low rumbling, like distant thunder. But it grew ever louder, to the tumble of an avalanche, to the crack and crash of two great icebergs coming together.

And then Leif found that he had stopped. That they had all three of them stopped, and turned, to see the grave-hills growing, gushing like earthen geysers, like three rippling volcanoes rising, rising – a dormant giant shrugging loose his shoulders and straightening his back.

It was a solid wall of earth, high as a hill behind them, and from the far side there came only yelps and whines as the Hunt found its path blocked.

'How long till they find a way around it?' said Astrid.

'Who knows? Enough, perhaps?' said Jaska. She was whispering, awed. Even Astrid looked impressed. But then she pulled herself together. 'It's bought us time,' she said. 'Now we must reach the temple.'

It lay before them in a low valley. And they rode into it, as if into a dream. Or into a nightmare.

CHAPTER NINETEEN

The moon's glare flashed white from a high roof, towering, broad. Though still far from them, it must be made of metal, to shine like that in even so little light. But between that beacon and themselves lay a wood of enormously tall trees. Stately, even godly figures, sylvan sentinels.

'Like Jelling's grove, before they cut it down,' said Leif.

Astrid sniffed. She had caught the scent of something on the wind. Something bad.

'More like Jelling was than you know,' she said, and her mind went back to that sticky spring day, long blocked from her mind, when Knut had sought her help in making the sacrifices.

Their horses slowed as they neared the trees. For all their haste, none of them quite wanted to stray into their shadows, under their branches. The spreading dark might swallow them whole.

'Come on,' said Jaska. 'They're only trees.' And she spurred her reluctant mount onwards.

Leif's flesh crept as they entered the grove, his hackles rising. He had heard tell of Uppsala as a place of dance and song, drinking and joking and merry celebration. This was different, a strange and spectral glade where your mind played tricks, so you thought you saw shapes spinning and twisting in the trees; shadows that looked like men or beasts, when they could only be broken branches.

He looked more closely. They *were* men and beasts. Swinging from rope ends.

Each tree bore its own strange fruit. They crowded in on him, swinging close, swinging clear. Birds. Cattle. Dogs. Horses. *Men.*

'So many dead,' whispered Jaska. 'I knew your people were cruel, but –' she could say no more.

'We don't do this,' said Astrid. 'Animals, yes – I always hated that – but never to each other. This is all wrong.'

'This is not the faith of our people,' said Leif. 'No more than were the stones near Trelleborg.' The bodies were bloated, flyblown, eyes bulging. *Wrong, wrong, wrong.*

'Faster,' said Astrid. 'We must get out of this place.'

Soon they had cleared the trees. Each felt a weight like a millstone lift from their backs – though it was none too pleasant to have those corpses behind you, knowing they were there but not looking at them. Who could tell if they dropped from their ropes and crept about when none was watching?

But before them the high walls of the temple were rising, separated from the dread wood that still spread to either side only by a gurgling spring, the water dark as oil and its music the sound of an uncanny chuckle. A demon or goblin might laugh like that: no water should.

'Jump it,' Astrid suggested, and they rode their horses over the broiling spring. No one dared think what might happen to the unlucky person who missed their step and fell into those black waters. It was clear now that the temple stood at the wood's centre, not its edge, and that the grim trees met on the far side, encircling them, closing them in. Not that it really mattered. But the thought of being hemmed in by all those silent swinging bodies made it at once a little harder to breathe.

'Some place for a last stand,' muttered Jaska.

If there was irony laced through her words, then Astrid missed it. 'You never said a truer word!' she gasped. She was looking at the temple.

It soared above them, and now they could all see plainly that its roof was wrought, not from iron, or even bronze, but from pure gold. Golden shingles fell in rows like the scales of a gargantuan dragon, high above their heads, and a thick gold chain dangled in loops from the gables like a maiden's tresses on high holiday. It was a fantastical place, like nothing any of them had ever seen. The sort of place a priest might dream into being, not a place that men would ever build. But there it was. Their final hope.

One tree alone stood beside the door, so tall that it overtopped the temple itself, its canopy spreading across the star-strewn sky. To their immense relief, no bodies dangled from its mighty branches. Its trunk was a sinuous great twisting of serpentine strands and weatherworn runnels. It was a yew tree.

Leif gaped. 'It might as well be Yggdrasil itself.' Never had he seen anything more like the World Tree, the centre of his faith and his imagination. It gave him courage.

'It's a weakness in our defences,' said Astrid. 'Except, I suppose, that wolves can't climb – even these ones?' No one knew. 'At least there's only one entrance,' she said. 'Inside! We've wasted enough time.' And she slipped off Hestur's back, and flung apart the golden doors.

⌐

'*Ow!* It's dark as Hel in here,' Astrid cursed, rubbing a stubbed toe. Not quite the grand entrance she had been hoping to make – at least no one could see her blushing.

'Leif, do that thing with the light. Hurry!'

All three were inside, dismounted, and Leif murmured a dim glow into existence. The first things they saw were braziers by the door, flints and oil, and a heavy wooden plank propped upright against the wall.

'First things first,' said Astrid. 'We must bar the door.'

It took all of them to lift the cold, massive beam. 'It must be bog oak,' Astrid grunted, but no one else could spare breath to reply. Finally it shuddered into place, resting in iron hooks riveted to the great golden doors, and they rubbed backs, mopped brows.

Jaska was the first to turn and see the kind of place they were in. So it was she who saw him first, and her scream rang clear through the sacred space.

He was sat in an oaken throne, garbed in chain mail, twice the height of any mortal man. The low green light of Leif's charm slid around and off his features, cold, evil. He leered at them with his one left eye.

'That's . . . that's *Odin*, isn't it?' Jaska said.

'It's only a statue,' said Astrid. 'No need to panic.'

'But,' said Jaska, 'but if he's *here* – I mean, if he's worshipped here – then isn't this still his kingdom? And this is no refuge, but a trap!'

'But we saw the Hunt ride upon the earth,' said Leif. 'If this were Odin's hall, they would have flown.'

'Torches!' said Astrid, and lit the two massive braziers, guttering red flame, spilling light around the hall. And the shadows unstuck themselves from the statue, and they all saw that it was not one god, but three, and Odin was simply the nearest.

Even Astrid was impressed. Three vast figures on three great thrones. In the centre was Thor, his beard full, his stone hammer in hand. The god of her eldest brother Knut, who had died in Ireland, and her mother Thyre, who had left her. It was some comfort to see him there, sat on high, but with a bite beneath the comfort. Like grit in porridge.

Odin sat at Thor's right hand. On the far side was Frey, god of the harvest and of birth, and he had been carved with a huge . . . Well, Astrid didn't really like to think about it. And as her eyes ran around the room, she saw more carvings, on pillars, on the walls – Njord, Freyja, Tyr, Heimdall and the rest – all the gods and goddesses of her faith.

'So Odin is but one of many here,' said Leif. 'And that explains why he wields no power. The Allfather fancies himself a king, and a king cannot rule among equals.'

'I like it,' said Jaska. 'All this magic here for you to draw on, so little of it his . . .'

Astrid turned away, irritated despite herself. They were only commoners; it wasn't fair to expect them to understand why you needed one strong ruler in a savage world. Someone to defend the helpless from attack. *From attack*. Why were they wasting time talking?

'Jaska,' she said. 'Check the windows; make sure there's no way in. Then I want you on watch.' She drew breath. 'Leif. Time to get thinking. We need a great poem. Your best.' He looked pale, Astrid thought. Tired. 'Remember . . . remember your hero, Egil Skallagrimsson. Remember the time he was a prisoner in England.' This was a story Leif himself had told her. 'He invented a poem that saved his life; that won his pardon from Erik Bloodaxe.' Of course, if the rumours were true, Erik Bloodaxe had been sort of her brother-in-law . . . She shook her head, angry at her inability to concentrate, and looked Leif in the eyes. 'We need a poem like that now.'

'Of course, Egil had a whole night to think,' said Leif.

She glowered at him. 'Then you'd better get started.' And she realised something. She was cross, tired, hungry. Her toe *really* stung. And – it would be stupid not to admit it – she was really rather scared. But more than that. This was the best she'd felt in ages. Perhaps since she'd stood in the prow of the *Klaastad* and sung down a storm, wrecked a ship. She was in charge. And whether this was really a last stand, or only Odin's way of testing her, it would be on her terms. She would show a god what she was made of. And more than that. She would show herself.

'*Show me, in blood, what is to be your will.*'

That was what he had said, the one-eyed god, when he offered her a place at his side, a life beyond death. Her will. Whatever it took, she *would* show him. Whatever it took.

↓

Firelight rippled from panels of beaten gold, snaked among high rafters. In one corner paced Leif, trying out phrases, kennings, alliteration. Around him, they had corralled the horses, nervous, big, powerful: the last line of defence. With every verse that fell into place, Leif was growing in confidence. The power of that place was seeping into him, the potency of ages, of a whole land. He could bring down a hunter and his pack, however terrible. Hadn't he bested an angel, after all?

Jaska was curled into a cramped window ledge. The only openings in the walls were thin arrow slits – perfect – enough to see by, not enough to let anyone in. And she had her bow strung, and a full quiver slung at her waist. Unblinking, she stared at the moon-washed grove, the way they had come: the spring, the open ground. Only the yew tree was out of sight. She'd have time for one, perhaps two shots, if they tried to rush the doors. She licked dry lips. Every moment, it was harder to see. Anything might be moving among those grim, dark trees, where the bodies swung and the shadows crept. A world slashed black and grey. A world that was waiting.

A world now streaked with rain. For Astrid was sat at the foot of the three statues, her harp in her lap. She had heard of too many hall-burnings to risk one here. Too many brave heroes denied their last fight by a canny enemy with a handful of torches. So she was playing the clouds into rain, wetting the hall, dampening the summer-dried timbers that supported the golden roof with a steady trickle of dancing minor chords.

The tune felt good. From the waist up, she was swaying now, entering the rhythm. Her fingers itched to take the tune on, and she let them lead her.

From high above, there came the low rumble of thunder.

Jaska looked up. 'Astrid!' she said. 'Careful. The rain will count for nothing if you bring a lightning strike down on our heads!'

Startled, Astrid flung down the harp. Jaska was right – she should know when to stop. But Jaska didn't know how it *felt*, to shape the skies, to weave the weather. Her head was a little giddy. Turning, she saw Thor, the thunder god, scowling down at her from his throne. Maybe she could have picked a better spot to sit . . .

'Jaska,' she said, getting up and stretching. 'Any sign?'

The girl shook her head, not turning from her window. 'Noth—' she began. But she left the word unfinished. They all felt it. Like a drenching in ice water.

'They're here,' said Astrid.

And deep in the dark wood, Grimnir the Grey blew a long low note on his horn. The Hunt had arrived.

157

CHAPTER TWENTY

Astrid wished for only one thing. All her life she had been trained to fight, playing with the jarls' little boys with wooden weapons, joining the would-be huscarls on the practice field, learning alongside her brothers. Few, she knew, could match her at her best, for she more than made up for any lack of strength with a speed and agility that was beyond bigger, heavier men.

But all her life, she had been trained with a sword and shield. She felt next to naked now, as she stood before the barred doors of the temple. Her limbs were slack, relaxed, her legs just shoulder-width apart, and she rolled back and forth, from the balls of her feet, to her toes, and back again. She was humming, softly, the echo of the rain-song she had played a moment before. Round her wrist, a leather thong was knotted, the other end made fast to the hilt of the Toledo blade that hung loose from her right hand. She was more ready for this than she'd ever been for anything.

But she wished she had a shield.

Her task, Astrid knew, was to protect Leif whilst he summoned the forces of Uppsala against the Hunt. It was the plan they had all made. But she didn't like it. Battles should be won with steel.

Above, Jaska was still perched, eyes fastened to the little window. She bit down on the rising lump of fear within her. As long as her hands didn't tremble, fear was fine. But if only she could *see*. Her instincts told her they were being watched – that there were eyes out there, hungry, baleful, fixed on their destruction. Killers lurking. But she could not see them, nor even tell the direction.

A glimpse, a flicker of movement – a paw, perhaps, or a tail, a low shape slipping between tree trunks. Off to the left. But then another blur, and a shadowy figure, away to the right. Were they being surrounded?

'Leif,' said Astrid. 'Are you ready?'

'I will be. But the Hunt must show itself,' came the reply. 'I cannot challenge those I cannot see.'

So they waited. And all the while, the wolves were circling.

ᚠ

'There!' breathed Jaska. A wolf had broken cover, at last, wriggling flat-bellied towards the spring. Without another word she notched an arrow, took aim, loosed it.

A yelp of pain. But as she drew again, the wolf whipped round and pelted, lopsided, back to the treeline, her arrow dangling from one forepaw. At the same time, figures stepped forward away to each side, drawing her eye, putting her off. They too turned and vanished, and her second arrow stayed unshot.

'A kill?' said Astrid.

'No,' said Jaska. 'A scratch. Sorry.'

'How many arrows have you got there?'

'Seven now.'

'Then don't waste any more. Make sure of your mark first.'

Jaska flushed. She knew all that. But she had been nervous, and had shot without being certain. The arrows were light, made to bring down small game, not Vargar. They would have to strike eye or heart.

And now the Hunt began to test her. One after another, a dark shape would melt out of the trees, darting, capering, returning to cover. Not trusting herself, she laid down her bow.

Not all looked quite like wolves. Whether it was because they had gone beyond Odin's power, or because this was no longer a chase but a siege, some of the Hunt had changed. Jaska tried to keep track of what she saw. It was made harder, because she could swear they were changing places, running to and fro out of sight, reappearing in different spots. But she was sure there were at least two true wolves, huge and dark, long-muzzled, hunch-shouldered. And two, maybe three, that had stuck somewhere in between man and wolf, rearing on two furry legs, dropping back to four – long, clawed hands, pointed, whiskered faces. Twitching tails. These were worse by far. If one of those things touched her . . .

And then there came a time when she saw none of the Vargar. Not a shadow stirred. It lasted so long that she felt her eyelids drooping, growing heavy. Had she dropped off? Missed something? In a panic, she pinched her bare left forearm, angry red welts forming on the soft white skin.

That was the moment the grey spearman stepped forth. All at once, Grimnir was there, high on the black horse, on the edge of the trees. And behind, from the corpse wood, there rose an eerie music. The pack was singing.

ᚾ

It rose and rose, the hunters' song, as if the wolves wanted to claw down the moon. The three listeners tensed, and Astrid had to fight the impulse of her own muscles to stop herself crouching, as if ready for flight. It was savage, grating, like the clash and scrape of metal on metal. But it was beautiful too, haunting, timeless, weird dissonance on the very edge of harmony. It was a sound pacing the line of order and chaos.

It rose so loud it filled the temple, filled their ears, so that only Jaska, higher up as she was, could make out a quiet scrabbling rustle in the rafters, higher still. Pigeons, or bats, she supposed, spooked by the howling. She would not let herself be distracted by meaningless noises. Not when she had to keep the Hunt in view.

ᚦ

And then they came, fast.

CHAPTER TWENTY-ONE

'He's charging!' cried Jaska.

The grey rider had spurred his horse and was coming on full tilt, clearing the spring, straight for the doors.

'They're running close behind!' said Jaska. The wolves and wolf-men were a streak of midnight in his wake. 'I count four!' she added, and, despite herself, loosed off an arrow at Grimnir. He was so close.

The shaft struck him full in the chest. It fell away in splinters.

And he came on, never checking, not even noticing the blow.

'Four?' said Astrid.

Then the black horse struck the golden doors with a crack to split the heavens, to split heads – and to split the bog-oak beam. The golden doors juddered apart, and first Astrid saw the steaming breath, the yellowed teeth, the big black nostrils of the maddened horse. Its small red eyes, massive shoulders, deadly hoofs. Astrid braced herself, shifting her fingers on the sword-hilt.

Then the doors swung wide and there was the grey hunter from Hedeby, towering above her. He raised his spear arm and, fixing her with that one malevolent eye – *How has he lost an eye?* – gestured past her, pointing the weapon. The Vargar surged in past him, a tide around a rock.

'Leif! *Now!*' Astrid screamed, and thrust at the nearest wolf. Snarling, it turned the point aside with a paw-swipe, barrelling past her. So close. No room to swing. They were jostling her arms, squeezing her between hot, hairy bodies. Trapped . . . stifled . . . no air . . .

Leif took a deep breath. He was ready, for he had discovered, he thought, the real shape of the world. Had found its pattern and its battle in the kindness of Johanna Svensdottir, in the words of his Huldra, and between the throttling fingers of Ginnarr the slaver, tightening round his neck. It was not about good against evil, as some Christians had it. Nor even order against chaos, as he had always learnt.

Nor was it the old gods against the new: the Odin of the Wild Hunt, Folkmar's god of vengeance and judgement, even Haralt Bluetooth himself – they were all the same.

And he, Leif, stood against them, along with every deer laid low by the hunter, every tree that knew the bite of the woodsman's axe, every blade of grass trampled underfoot. Everyone ever threatened by the pointing of a spear.

He would stand against that spear, and speak it into submission. It would be an elegy for Issar.

It would be the poem of his life.

So he took a deep breath. Filled his lungs. Moistened his lips.

And the fifth Vargur dropped from the rafters behind him, and clapped a hairy paw across his mouth.

Astrid was spun by the pressing, rushing bodies, struggling to free her right elbow, aim a blow. Blindsided, she never saw the flailing hoof that caught her in the back, knocked her to the ground. The sword flew from her grasp, the leather thong biting deep into her wrist as it went. She scrabbled on the floor, desperately seeking the blade. Above was a terrible confusion of noise, grunting and thumping . . . *There!* The touch of cold steel, the wicked edge. Reaching along it, fumbling for the hilt.

And her hand came to rest upon a human foot.

Looking up, she saw the grey hunter, dismounted, staring down at her.

‡

The noises had stopped. All was still, and quiet. As after the rain.

No screams. That was something. No verses either, no moving of elements and shifting of the world's fabric, no magic being worked by Leif's words. So. He had failed.

Glaring, Astrid came to her feet. It was torture to tear her eyes from that grim, silent figure, who still loomed well above her head even now. But she risked a swift glance around the room, a harsh, animal jerk of the head to either side.

Leif was pinned, struggling, in the grip of a hideous, wolf-headed form, like a grotesque imitation of a man, long-limbed and thick-furred, one lean grey arm locked round Leif's chest, the other closed over his mouth.

It was when Jaska had shouted 'I count four!' that Astrid's stomach had swooped; that she had known something was going to go wrong.

And there was Jaska, on the ground, flattened by a heavy dog-wolf, squat muzzle, slavering jaws. Was she breathing? Astrid could see no blood. And then Jaska moaned.

They were all alive.

Why?

She had, she remembered, a knife at her waist, a quick little blade in a leather sheath. It would be the work of a moment to draw it. But there was the hunter before her, and a Vargur pressing close on either side. And at her back, the great statue of Odin.

She thought that she could hear it breathing.

ᚠ

'*The Hunt is at an end.*' It was Odin's voice, and it was all around her, echoing off the pillars, doors, roof, and Astrid didn't dare turn to see if it was the statue that was speaking, if it had come to life. Then there was no sound but the steady drip of water, though it had stopped raining.

Astrid glanced up. There was a hole in the golden roof, and water was running in. Beyond it, she saw only branches. *The yew tree*, she thought. She'd known it was a weakness. The fifth of the Vargar must have climbed it, made the hole, taken Leif unawares. They had failed.

Perhaps, now it was over, and Odin had proved he could win, the game would end with mercy. Was that why no blood had been shed? Because they were all to be let go, humbled? And, if so, did that make her relieved? Or ashamed?

'No,' rumbled the god's voice, a voice like her father's. 'I know many things. Almost all. But mercy is not one of them.'

He had heard her thoughts.

'Of course,' he said. 'Have I not been in your head for many nights now? Are we not as close as kin?'

There was a stir, a gasp from Jaska, and Astrid realised that the voice really *was* filling the temple. They could hear every word. That meant it almost certainly *was* the statue. But still, she kept her eyes riveted on the man before her. The man with the spear.

'If I have let them live,' said Odin, 'it is not from charity. The Hunt is at an end. Now comes the bloodletting. The sacrifice.'

And Grimnir moved before her. Instinctively she flinched away. Then she blinked. He was holding out his spear.

'Take it,' came the voice. Astrid goggled.

'The Hunter is merely my vessel. A part of me. And a god cannot sacrifice to himself. It must be done by a mortal's hand. So take it.'

And still she didn't understand.

ᚱ

Leif continued to writhe in the creature's iron grip. Its limbs were rough and scratchy on his flesh. Its stench was indescribable. But he had to keep his nostrils wide to breathe, with that awful paw clamped tight across his mouth.

'*Be glad,*' the Vargur whispered in his ear, '*that I haven't ripped out your tongue by the roots.*' The voice itself was worse than the words. Leif shivered.

Astrid seemed to be talking to the other voice, Odin's voice, that came from the speaking statue. Only its lips were moving – which was something, he supposed. What the god meant about their closeness, he didn't care to guess. But he understood about the spear all right. Really, sometimes, Astrid was so stupid. It was almost endearing.

If only he could speak, he could tell her. This temple, this site of worship, was a source of vast power. Like Jelling. He had felt it from the first. But no one god could lay claim to that power: the sacrifices were split. Men prayed and killed in the name of many, and Odin had no more right than Frey or Thor to say that he ruled here. All those bodies, hanging in the grove – they too must be dedicated evenly between the three gods.

But if more were killed, here, in the temple itself . . . If blood were spilt in Odin's name alone, to end the Wild Hunt, then the balance would tip, and Uppsala would belong only to the Allfather.

No wonder they hadn't been killed yet. Their blood was too valuable to waste. But there was only one way for Odin to make it his.

It had to be Astrid who did it.

CHAPTER TWENTY-TWO

'*Take it,*' said the voice. '*And show me, in blood, what is to be your will. You can die, here, with them. Unlamented, unimportant. Your death will serve no purpose. The Hunt will take its prey, that is all.*' A pause. '*Or, you can make the sacrifice. Prove yourself. And then, shield maiden, you will be welcome to ride at my side for the rest of time.*'

Astrid stared. Unflinching, unmoving, the one-eyed hunter stared back.

'*You want it,*' Odin said, and the words stroked, softly, around the hall. '*Why else would you have helped the Hunt this long? Why else lead us here?*'

Jaska let out a cry, tried to rise. The squat-nosed wolf leant its whole weight upon her, pressing her back to the ground.

'*You hid it from them well, little princess, just as you first hid your lineage: daughter of Gorm the Old, the Lapp didn't know that, just as, at Birka, they didn't know why you were followed, attacked, by Haralt Bluetooth's warriors. You are a liar after my own heart: one who lies by saying nothing, rather than too much. Some of it you have not dared say even to yourself.'*

And this time it was Leif who fought to be free. Fought and failed.

'The first sign was fated. The raven feather that fell from your dress, when you rode away from the lakeside. The mark of your encounter with my emissary – and even that meeting, you kept well hidden from your companions.'

Leif tried, wildly, to bite down on the paw that stifled him. In response, cruel claws dug under his ribs, raking down. He gave up.

'But the second sign was of your own devising. The broken branch, beside the frozen river. When my hunters were ready to give up all hope. You showed them the trail.'

Astrid swallowed hard.

'And the third time, Gormsdottir, as all seemed lost. When your companions had spent the last of their courage, their trickery, to mask the scent and sweep the path once more. By the Vargur's dead body, it was you who hung back and carved the runes: the runes that led us here. You wanted this as much as I. Desired this ending. Hungered for it. The wolf is in you too; you cannot deny it. You were born and bred to hunt, not to be hunted. So take the spear. And finish this thing.'

Dumbly, as if in a dream, Astrid stretched out her hand. Took the spear from Grimnir.

The Vargur holding Leif lifted him bodily into the air. Its strength was appalling. Then it lurched with a weird, animal gait over to Odin's statue, and shoved the boy against the god's massive, carved feet.

A memory flashed through Leif's head. The ordeal, at Jelling, in the stone circle. The knife in his hand, Folkmar helpless before him. He had shown mercy then, he had thought. But was it just that he had been a coward? Too afraid to spill blood?

Astrid was no coward.

He glanced up at her, standing before him. Her stance was that of a killer. Alert. Potent. Perfectly balanced. She had never seemed so far from him as in that moment. Was it only now that he had lost her, he wondered? Or before? In that terrible forest, as they grew ever further apart?

He wanted her to know that he understood; that he knew, and that he forgave. He tried to put it all in his eyes as she raised the spear, testing its weight. For an instant, their eyes locked. But his skill had always been in words, not looks, and he wasn't sure she could tell what he meant. Maybe, after all, he just looked afraid. A coward to the end.

Astrid's lips parted in a murmur. Straining, he just made out the words. 'Iceland or anywhere,' she said. And of all the anywheres, he just had time to think, who would have thought their journey would lead them, at the last, to here?

Then he closed his eyes, and she drove the spear home.

CHAPTER TWENTY-THREE

'Iceland or anywhere,' breathed Astrid, and she drove the spear home. She was aiming up, under the ribcage, at the heart, and she was surprised at how much effort it took. Flesh is soft, but solid, and it clings to a spear's metal tip, so you try to twist it, and then you lose your aim. Her upper arms burnt and strained, the sweat sprung forth on her brow and on her back, but she used her whole body, pushing from the heels, and she felt the vibrations run down the shaft and tremor her hands, and felt the moment when the iron bit the heart.

It was the hardest thing she'd ever done.

Grimnir sighed. Soft as goose down. He looked at Astrid, and then at the spear, and for the first time, she thought his face was happy. Almost human. And then he toppled over backwards, a great grey body crashing to the ground, and there was pandemonium in the hall.

The two Vargar flanking Astrid lunged at her with howls of rage. She was no longer there, throwing herself after the fall of Grimnir's body, snatching her sword from beneath him. She hit the floor, hard, and winced as her shoulder and knees took the blow. But already she was pushing up, twisting round, the point of her blade on guard against the wolf-men.

The other three beasts were rushing at her, rushing to where their master lay in a growing pool of bile and blood. One never got that far. Jaska, arms freed as the brute rose above her, had her knife drawn in an instant. Before she could think about what she was doing, she had run its point along the exposed belly overhead, slitting it open, and writhed quickly to one side as the wolf collapsed.

Leif opened his eyes to see Astrid diving aside, two massive beasts on their hind legs clashing above her, two more hurling themselves her way. She was up again, the sword a dance of silver in her hand, her hair a wild swirl of gold, and there was fire in her eyes. She was almost too beautiful to look at.

He came to his feet, flinging an arm forward, pointing.

'He who tries to harm her
Touches the rising sun!'

The air around her bloomed with white-hot light, and now he did have to shield his eyes. The two two-legged Vargar were committed, lunging at Astrid, and they plunged into a halo of white fire. She met them without flinching, passing the sword clean through the body of one and swiftly withdrawing, and with a single downswipe, she cleaved the head from the other as it fell past her, burning.

The fourth wolf was coming now, rushing at her from behind, but Jaska had snatched up her bow, hands sticky with guts and blood and slime, and an arrow blossomed from the wolf's neck as it fell.

The final wolf never broke its stride, but arced its body in a desperate sideways leap. Sparks flew from its fur, and there was a horrible smell of singed hair, but it made it past the circle of sun-fire and, yowling, pelted out of the golden doors. Jaska dashed after it.

'Let it go,' said Astrid. 'It's only an animal, now.'

They turned to her. The deadly fire no longer blossomed forth. But it was still there, in her stance, in her eyes, playing behind the shaping of her smile.

'I'm back,' she said. 'It's over. How long I've been away. But I'm back now.' Outside, the real sun was rising.

CHAPTER TWENTY-FOUR

They carried Grimnir's body to the spring. It seemed right to give him to the flowing, crystal waters, no longer dark with night. The sky had cleared with the coming of day, and blue and gold danced freely in the stream. Perhaps it would clean him, soothe him, bathe his tortured spirit.

'Are we dedicating this to anyone?' said Jaska, as they heaved the great corpse in.

Astrid shook her head. 'No more sacrifices.'

And they lingered on the bank, beneath the tree. No one wanted to go back into that hall, with its blood-spattered floor, where four bodies still lay. Where Odin's statue now wore an ugly scowl.

Astrid told them the story. Slowly, quietly. The raven; the dreams of the one-eyed god.

'"Show me, in blood, what is to be your will,"' Leif quoted. He paused. Shook his head. 'What a will.'

†

Later, he laid a hand on her arm. 'Astrid, you'd be an awful Valkyrie,' he said.

She frowned at him. Opened her mouth. He held a finger to her lips. 'I mean, you were never meant to *follow*. Eternity, spent serving an old man? No, Astrid. You'll always be a leader.'

She smiled then. 'You know, I wish Issar were here to watch the sun rise,' she said, and Leif gave a tight little nod. There still weren't the words. And, after a while, 'You never really thought I'd do it, did you? Stick a spear in my best friend? I mean, of course Odin's offer was tempting. But that was where he went wrong, don't you see? A choice like that, put so plainly . . . well, that's no choice at all.'

She was looking at the ground though, not meeting his eyes. Leif felt a lump in his throat. Instead of trying to answer, he just squeezed her palm. As if there were no need for words. It was easier that way.

It was warm on the bank, midmorning, late summer. Jaska stretched, cat-lazy, in the sun. 'I hate myself for even asking this,' she said, 'because I want to lie here and doze for ever and ever. But . . . I mean, the Hunt's over. And we're still here. We can't go back to Birka. So – what are we going to do now?' And she looked, quite naturally, to Astrid. Astrid was their leader.

'Well,' Astrid said, pushing a stray strand of hair from her forehead, 'I'm going to need a new plait . . .' She smiled, though the smile never reached her eyes. She wasn't comfortable, not here, with bodies in the temple behind, bodies in the grove in front. Small deaths in the service of great gods. And though *this* Hunt was over, might another not still be on? They had tried to start a new life, and been hounded right out to here, in the back end of nowhere. Would Haralt send more men? Would Odin? And she was done with running, that much she did know.

Leif thought he heard a gentle rustle in the bole of the yew tree. Glancing up through shaded eyes, he half imagined he saw his Huldra, standing in the shadows. He wasn't sure what to think about her, and about Astrid, any more. That moment, when he had seen Astrid, and she had been the sun! But he knew the two could never meet. They were different worlds.

Astrid scratched the healing wound at the back of her head. There was nothing for them here. There was nowhere left to run. What happened when the Hunting had its end?

She looked around at her two friends. At their expectant faces. And she smiled with her whole being, a second sun arisen, as she said, 'We're going home.'

HISTORICAL NOTE

This book isn't quite as true as the last one. The bishops are real, as well as the geography and the places – Birka, Hedeby, and the stone circle at Hunnestad, sadly no longer standing. And the wreck of an ancient vessel was recently found in the sands west of Trelleborg. But *The Wild Hunt* is more about true myth than truth, and about the power of telling tales. How what was said became more important than what *was*. So neither Reginbrand of Aarhus nor Ibrahim ibn Yaqub (if Issar really was Leif's father) actually died in a Swedish forest. But instead we have the folklore and the legends from the Sami and the Old Norse – Jaska's fevered dreams, the Huldra, the Vargar and, of course, the Hunt itself. Grimnir is dogged by rumours of sacrifices that we get from Thietmar of Merseburg. Above all we have the incredible (except to the credulous) account of the Great Temple at Uppsala, and the sacrifices performed there, taken from the writings of Adam of Bremen. People put all sorts of nonsense in books. This one is no exception.

ACKNOWLEDGEMENTS

Thank you, again. To the ruthless, passionate Emma Matthewson, the dizzyingly competent Jenny Jacoby, and the eagle eyes of Catherine Coe (how I have come to trust your way with a semicolon!). To the judgement (plotting) and generosity (lunching) of Christopher Little, the savviness of Stephanie Thwaites, and the all-round brilliance of Jules Bearman. To family, friends, and colleagues all (to particularise between whom it would be invidious etc) but especially my parents, for pedantry and impatience (the good sort), Freyja for aesthetic sense and cool cynicism, and Emma for more unpaid perusing. This book is for Charlie Sangster, the best Viking I ever knew.

OSKAR JENSEN

When not writing novels about Norsemen (and women), playing five-a-side football or various instruments, Oskar moonlights (full-time) as a postdoctoral researcher in the Music Department of King's College London. It's all very confusing. Having squandered years of writing on student journalism, and, even worse, student poetry, most of his literary efforts are now either academic, or songs, or both. Find out more at oskarjensen.com

HOT
KEY
BOOKS

Thank you for choosing a Hot Key book.

If you want to know more about our authors and what we publish, you can find us online.

You can start at our website

www.hotkeybooks.com

And you can also find us on:

We hope to see you soon!